THE
GIRL WHO BUILT
A SPIDER

GEORGE BREWINGTON

GODWIN BOOKS
HENRY HOLT AND COMPANY
NEW YORK

Henry Holt and Company, *Publishers since 1866*
Henry Holt® is a registered trademark of Macmillan Publishing Group, LLC
120 Broadway, New York, NY 10271 • mackids.com

Our books may be purchased in bulk for promotional, educational, or business use. Please
contact your local bookseller or the Macmillan Corporate and Premium Sales Department
at (800) 221-7945 ext. 5442 or by email at MacmillanSpecialMarkets@macmillan.com.

Library of Congress Cataloging-in-Publication Data is available.

First edition, 2023
Book design by L. Whitt
Printed in the United States of America by Sheridan, Brainerd, Minnesota

ISBN 978-1-250-16580-0 (hardcover)

1   3   5   7   9   10   8   6   4   2

FOR JAMES,
WHO LOVES ROBOTS

CHAPTER ONE
THE MYSTERY GUEST

Theresa Brown never thought her solar-powered mechanical spider would win the Charleston County Middle School Science Fair, but it did. You could sit in its central rotating seat, move in any direction, carry an additional passenger, climb over any obstacle, and when you were ready to put it away, you could fold its eight double-jointed legs together so that it was no bigger than a suitcase.

All five judges gave it a try. It was really quite something.

Theresa's spider even beat out Ashley Dean's edible algae that provided you all your daily nutrients with a single serving but unfortunately tasted like dirt. Everyone had assumed Ashley would take first place. After all, she was the student body president of Daniel Island Middle School *and* a straight A student *and* very well-spoken. She had explained the benefits of her spirulina superfood to the five judges very clearly. But Ashley's algae took second.

Third place went to Jon Cooper's durable bubble maker. At first look, Jon seemed to have the laziest invention of all—a Hula-Hoop and an inflatable pool full of what appeared to be soapy water. But the solution was a biodegradable liquid plastic that clung to the hoop, and when Jon placed a fan in front of it, he could wave the hoop and make bubbles of all shapes and sizes that didn't pop unless you really took a whack at them with a stick. They were fun to play with, and Jon certainly was enthusiastic about them. He even showed the science fair crowd that he could fully encase himself inside a bubble, despite his mother's warnings that he would suffocate.

The five judges were science teachers from various middle schools throughout the county. They were all in a bit of a hurry, scrambling to organize the winners on the outdoor stage because dark and threatening storm clouds were brewing over the harbor. A tropical storm was expected to make landfall within hours, and a very important mystery guest had yet to arrive.

The first judge was a teacher representing Theresa's school— James Island Middle. She handed Theresa, Ashley, and Jon their blue, red, and white ribbons respectively.

The second judge placed Theresa, Jon, and Ashley on a tiered podium like the ones at the Olympics ceremonies. Theresa, of course, stood in the middle for first place. She towered over Ashley and Jon as she looked out at the heads of all the people in the audience. She felt *very* awkward. She

immediately wished she hadn't worn her *Aladdin* T-shirt, blue jeans, and a plastic Princess Jasmine bow in her hair. She thought she must look like a little kid next to Ashley, who stood very tall with her chin up and not one hair out of place. Ashley had decided to wear a blue dress with smart white stripes like she *knew* she was going to win.

To Theresa, Ashley seemed smarter and cooler than her. She guessed Ashley was *really* popular at her school. Theresa certainly didn't feel like she belonged on the stage next to her, momentarily forgetting that *she* was the one holding the blue ribbon, *not* Ashley.

Jon was less intimidating. He was wearing his yellow T-shirt inside out. She wondered if he had done that on purpose. And what was he doing with his tongue? He seemed to have just discovered he had one. He darted it in and out of his mouth like an iguana.

The third judge tested the stage microphone for reverb. She said, "Testing, testing. One, two, three. Hello, everybody!"

The fourth judge asked all family and friends of the contestants to take their seats. Then Theresa was *really* embarrassed. Her father hadn't come. Of course, he hadn't for a very good reason—he had no idea she was here.

The fifth judge went behind the purple backdrop curtain of the stage in hopes of finding the mystery guest, who was now indisputably late.

Theresa stared at the tops of all the heads, trying to stand as still as she could. There must have been more than two

hundred parents, grandparents, and teachers there, all looking at her.

Everyone began to murmur.

Who is the mystery guest? Who cares if the guest is found or not? Can't the kids give their thank-you speeches now so we can just go home? It's sure to rain any minute!

Theresa really needed to scratch her back, but she didn't dare. Jon, on the other hand, kept giggling, sticking out his tongue, and waving to his older brothers and sisters in the third row. Jon was the youngest of eight.

Three large news cameras for Channels 2, 4, and 5 appeared right in front of the podium. A reporter hurried up next to Theresa and asked if she was excited. She was too petrified to say anything, so Ashley leaned into the microphone and said, "I'm very honored to be here. Thank you to Charleston's outstanding science teachers for making this event possible. It's a such *wonderful* day for all of us."

Theresa wished she had said that.

Finally, the remaining four judges huddled together and agreed they couldn't wait any longer. The wind was picking up, and the clouds above them were growing increasingly black. The third judge turned to speak into the microphone.

"Ladies and gentlemen, we apologize for the delay. We are so proud of this year's young scientists. There were so many wonderful inventions on display, we found it quite difficult to pick only three. But somehow, scoring for ingenuity, uniqueness, and display, we picked the very *best* of the best.

We wanted to wait for our special guest, who was going to make an incredible, amazing, once-in-a-lifetime offer to our first-place winner, Theresa Brown, but I guess—Oh, wonderful! He's here!"

Theresa didn't have time to think. What offer? No one had said anything about an offer. She probably shouldn't have signed up for this science fair in the first place. An offer might get her in deep trouble.

Suddenly, the purple backstage curtain flew open in a flurry, and the news cameras immediately turned in that direction.

A tall, broad-shouldered man with wild brown eyes and a rebellious mop of black-and-white curls on his head strode past the fifth judge onto the stage in a huff, as if he believed that *he* wasn't late but everyone else *was*. He was wearing a pink T-shirt, rubber wading boots that went past his knees, and a pair of white overalls with many more pockets sewn onto them than the designer originally intended. His boots were caked in pluff mud—the sticky, gooey, almost-like-quicksand black mud of South Carolina's marshes. He must have been out collecting oysters or bugs or who knows what.

But his clothes were certainly not as arresting as the metal headband he wore.

Three glowing tubes connected to the headband writhed atop his head like cobras, each seeming to probe the air for something. One was blue, one was green, and one was red. Theresa felt hypnotized by them and for good reason—all three tubes were slowly turning toward her.

Before the judge could offer him a seat, he took one of the folding chairs and sat right next to the tiered podium, nodding a greeting to Theresa, Ashley, and Jon.

Ashley nodded back politely and professionally. Jon outright laughed and waved for his seven siblings' attention as he pointed excitedly to the three glowing snakes on the scientist's head. Poor Theresa didn't know what to do, because the wiggling tubes suddenly grouped together and pointed at her in unified formation, emitting a startling, incriminating beep every three seconds. The beeping almost sounded like, *YOU! YOU! YOU!*

Theresa felt guilty for something, but she had no idea what.

The fifth judge stepped proudly up to the microphone.

"Ladies and gentlemen! Our mystery guest has been found! Please join me in welcoming Charleston's greatest scientist—the inventor of the Bionic Baby Bottom Buffer—Dr. Neil Flax!"

CHAPTER TWO
I CAN BUILD THINGS

All five judges sighed with relief as the first judge returned to the microphone.

"Thank you for joining us, Dr. Flax. Now, without further ado, it is my honor to congratulate Jon Cooper, Ashley Dean, and our first-place winner, Theresa Brown, for their fascinating projects. How about we let each of them tell us what inspired them to create such wonderful inventions? Then we'll let Dr. Flax announce his incredible, amazing, once-in-a-lifetime offer to Theresa."

She handed the microphone to Jon.

Theresa began to sweat. She had *no* desire to talk about what had inspired her. In her head, she began to make up a simple and acceptable speech. Something about her love of spiders or mechanical things or whatever.

Jon didn't mind speaking at all.

"I love bubbles. Bubbles are awesome! My bubbles are the

best bubbles on the planet, and I'm going to make them even bigger next time!"

Dr. Flax chuckled and snorted at Jon's enthusiasm, which seemed to give the rest of the audience permission to laugh out loud.

Ashley took the microphone out of Jon's hand.

"Thank you very much for this opportunity," she said in her most serious voice. "I want to thank the judges and especially Dr. Flax for coming today. I was inspired to create a food source that would be easy to grow and replicate in large amounts because so many people are starving unnecessarily. Did you know that one in seven people in the world does not have enough food to eat in a day? That's 795 million people. Right here in South Carolina, 680,000 people go hungry every day, and 200,000 of those are children. I think we can do better. As our planet suffers the effects of a dramatically changing climate, we need to have more plentiful food sources that can adapt effectively. Ashley Dean's Edible Algae will be one of those critical food sources, and I plan to invent many, many more. Thank you very much."

The audience clapped loudly, as did Dr. Flax. Ashley bowed graciously. She really knew how to give a good speech. Luckily for Ashley, she couldn't hear Jon over the loud applause when he said, "Tastes like dirt, though."

Ashley handed the microphone to Theresa with a daring look that seemed to say, *Beat that.*

Theresa took the microphone. But she couldn't stop looking

at the glowing tubes on Dr. Flax's head. They had pointed themselves directly at her. Seeing her hesitation, the famous scientist leaned forward and spoke to her quietly.

"This headband has proven to be one of my most useful inventions, Miss Brown. I call it my External Lie Detector. Without needing physical contact with the suspect, the red tube listens for a rapid heart rate, the blue tube watches for a high respiratory rate, and the green tube smells out those who are sweating excessively. You are guilty of all three, so my three snakey friends like you very much."

"But I haven't even said anything," Theresa whispered with her hand over the microphone.

Dr. Flax smiled coyly. "But you *are* hiding something, aren't you? Your heart is pounding, you're breathing quite quickly, and I see drops of sweat forming on your forehead. Perhaps you didn't build that wonderful spider by yourself. It seems an awfully complicated machine for a twelve-year-old girl to design and weld together all on her own. If you have not been completely forthcoming about your invention, now would be a good time to say so."

Ashley smirked and Jon giggled as every passing awkward moment made Theresa appear all the more guilty of *not* building the mechanical spider that was her greatest pride and joy.

Her shyness was quickly replaced with anger.

She *had* built the spider herself. The plastic parts for the joints she had programmed into her 3D printer. The aluminum for the legs and the base she had taken from old cars

from her uncle Robert's auto repair shop. He had taught her to weld when she was only five, so she had gotten pretty good at making whatever she could imagine from scrap.

The only parts of the spider she hadn't built herself were the solar-powered battery (which she had bought for twenty dollars at a flea market) and the rotating seat (which she had unscrewed off a lawn tractor). She couldn't believe this crazy-haired scientist in muddy overalls who didn't even have the decency to show up on time would imply that she was a liar and a fraud. All because some glowing tubes on his head said so?

Despite her stage fright, Theresa decided to show this so-called scientist and his lie-detecting tiara just what the truth sounded like.

Theresa rolled her shoulders back and spoke into the microphone.

"My name is Theresa Brown. I was born and raised in South Carolina, and I built this spider *all by myself.* What inspired me? I don't know. My dad doesn't let me leave the house much ever since my mother drowned in a flood caused by a Category 5 hurricane. He doesn't even know I'm here. I was only three years old when we lost her. There's been a black hole inside me ever since. And my dad is still scared of storms. I suppose I am, too. So I spend a lot of time alone playing with robots, which lets me forget about storms and the black hole inside me—at least for a while. I wish I could do something about hurricanes."

Theresa turned from the crowd to face Dr. Flax in his chair and spoke directly to him with hot fury in her eyes.

"But even though I might not be able to do anything about hurricanes, I *can* build things. I've always been good at welding and putting together motors and making stuff with my 3D printer. No matter what your lie detector says, I designed and built this spider *all by myself*. Hurricanes are getting bigger and scarier, and I'm frustrated and sad that my mother's gone, and I wish my dad didn't get so anxious every time it rained, but at least I have my spider. She makes me happy. So I snuck out of the house even though a storm is coming, which will totally freak out my dad. But it feels pretty good to see my spider win first place. She's the most beautiful machine I've ever built. So thank you very much to the judges, I guess, for giving her a blue ribbon."

Theresa placed the microphone on the podium and fought every urge to run off the stage. More than anything at that moment, she wanted to be alone.

But then she saw Dr. Flax quietly nodding as if he were very, very impressed. The tubes on his headband had recoiled into three spiral buns and rested quietly in the nest of wild curls on top of his head.

The peculiar scientist stood up and scratched his cheek as he studied Theresa, as if he had completely forgotten about the audience and the news reporters. After a whole minute, Dr. Flax picked up the microphone and spoke.

"Thank you very much, Miss Brown," he said with a smile. "That was quite an honest answer."

Then he remembered there was a large audience behind him and turned to speak to them.

"Yes, it is true, everybody, I am Dr. Neil Flax, the inventor of the Bionic Baby Bottom Buffer."

Loud applause followed, but the doctor put his hand up for quiet.

"Fine, very fine, and I thank you. Yes, everyone loves my automatic baby diaper changer and baby bum wiper. I'm glad I could make life easier for parents all around the world. That invention earned me a whole lot of money, which allowed me to build the laboratory of my dreams.

"With my dream laboratory, I'd like to do something bigger and better than polish baby behinds. The *world* needs something bigger. Miss Dean is quite right. Our planet *is* going through dramatic changes, and we must do better for her. Hurricanes grow stronger, fires and floods have become more frequent, and as Miss Brown unfortunately knows, more and more of our loved ones are lost."

Dr. Flax turned to give Theresa a heartfelt smile that made her feel so self-conscious, she was sure her face was as red as a tomato.

"Sometimes we feel like the world is ending," Dr. Flax continued. "We feel like there's nothing we can do. In fact, sometimes problems seem so big, we are tempted to decide they

are impossible to solve. Sometimes we even fool ourselves into thinking they aren't problems at all.

"But I am here to tell you fine people that no problem is too big for science! If we can put humans on the moon and submarines in our deepest oceans, *then we can fight hurricanes*. No matter how scary the world becomes, we must maintain the optimistic enthusiasm of Mr. Cooper here, who is going to make his bubbles bigger and better no matter what."

Jon smiled slyly, making sure his brothers and sisters were watching. Then he stuck out his tongue like a proud lizard. Dr. Flax chuckled softly and continued.

"So, Miss Brown, forgive me that I thought you might be hiding something. I admit, I find myself paranoid as of late. I must ensure that if I am to invite three aspiring inventors into my new dream laboratory, they must be trustworthy and with noble intention. So I beg your apology, Miss Brown."

"That's okay," Theresa said awkwardly. Ashley's eyes grew wide, and Jon laughed with excitement. Theresa wondered if her ears were working right. What did he just say?

Dr. Flax turned back to the microphone.

"So, an offer was mentioned! Here it is. Miss Brown, Miss Dean, Mr. Cooper, please consider yourselves invited to spend this summer in my laboratory to build the inventions of *your* dreams. If you succeed, and if any of your inventions shows potential to make the world a better place, then Flax

Industries will produce it and include it in next year's Flax Inventions for a Better World catalog. One of you might be the next Leonardo da Vinci, and goodness knows I want the next Da Vinci working for me. So let's work together to help save this planet, to slow climate change, and yes, Miss Brown, *to even stop hurricanes.*

"Sound good to everybody? Okay, great. Now I really must return to urgent business. See you tomorrow at nine. Bye-bye."

With that, Dr. Flax turned to exit, knocking over the microphone stand as he did. The crowd didn't know whether to clap as the second judge picked up the microphone.

"Pardon me, Dr. Flax?" the judge asked. "Did you say you're offering *all three* of our winners summer internships at Flax Industries?"

"I did indeed."

The doctor became quite flustered as he couldn't seem to find the opening in the purple backdrop curtain.

"Did you say they should come *tomorrow*? Because there are two and a half more weeks of school left!"

"The following Monday, then," the doctor said as he swatted at the curtain folds. "We will begin our day at nine and end at five. I'll provide a healthy and tasty lunch. Wear clothes you're not afraid to get dirty. Okay, I really must be leaving."

Then it began to rain. Hard.

Dr. Flax continued to struggle with the curtain, pushing it left and right as the rain poured down on all of them. The fifth judge stepped forward to help him. The audience began

to quickly disperse. Soon only Theresa, Ashley, and Jon were left watching the famous scientist and the judge struggle to find the exit. When they finally did, Dr. Flax gave the three winning students a fleeting smile, slid through the curtain folds, and was gone.

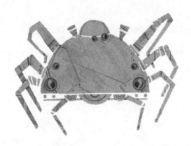

CHAPTER THREE
WHERE HAVE YOU BEEN?

Theresa drove her spider from downtown Charleston to Folly Road and all the way home along the bicycle lane to Folly Beach. Not many people have seen a girl riding a mechanical spider before, so drivers frequently pulled over to snap her photo with their phones. Bicyclists trying to escape the rain couldn't resist stopping to watch her drive by. Her spider's aluminum spindle legs ended in points, so as she drove along, the points clicked against the wet asphalt, tapping *clickety-clickety-click-click-clickety-clickety-click-click*.

At its top speed, her spider traveled at twelve miles an hour. Folly Beach roads often flooded during storms so that cars had to find another route or turn around altogether. But flooded roads were no matter for her spider's long legs. Theresa could march right through deep puddles, and if there was a fallen tree in the middle of the road, she could walk her spider over that, too.

When she finally arrived at home, it was past six o'clock. Theresa was soaked. She decided that one day she should install a retractable umbrella to the back of the spider's seat to keep herself dry.

Like many of the houses in Folly Beach, her home stood twelve feet above the ground on stilts to keep it safe from flooding caused by frequent hurricanes. Theresa unlocked the ground-floor door with a key tied around her neck. She folded up her spider's legs so that she could carry it through the door.

Her father was sitting at the top of the stairs waiting for her, even though he was supposed to be at the hospital.

"Theresa! Where have you been?"

By the dim light of the single bulb in the stairwell, she could see his thinning hair was pointing in three different directions from running his hands through it as he had been imagining the worst.

"I thought you were still at work, Dad," she said softly.

Her father was a nurse at Charleston City Hospital. He was still wearing his blue scrubs. He hurried down the stairs and held her tightly in his arms.

"I came home to prepare for the storm. You were supposed to stay inside. Do you know how worried I've been? You should have texted me. You should have called. You should never have left the house! Why would you scare me like that?"

He was talking so fast and squeezing her so hard, she wondered if she should even try to answer until he got all his worry out of his system.

"Theresa. Please tell me. *Where did you go?*"

"Well, first of all, let me start by saying it was a school-sponsored event—"

"Baby girl, do you see how the rain is coming down? This storm could become a full-fledged hurricane! There's so much to do! We need to check all the batteries in the emergency kit. We need to board up the windows and make ice and fill the tub with water—and—and—and all I could imagine was that you'd been caught in a—"

Then he turned away from her and put his head in his hands. Theresa knew why. Her mother's drowning wasn't his fault at all, but he blamed himself for it every day.

"I'm sorry, Dad" was all she could say, and she wrapped her arms around him and kissed his shoulder.

"These scrubs are dirty." He laughed, beginning—*finally*—to calm down.

"I know. I can't believe I just kissed them. Totally gross."

They both sat on the bottom stair, listening to the thunder cracking and the rain coming down.

Then, even though the wind was really shaking the windows, he took a deep breath and dared to ask:

"What school-sponsored event?" He sighed.

Theresa felt guilty. Maybe she shouldn't have snuck out of the house to enter a science fair when a storm was coming. But to be part of a contest where she could show off her creation was something she had wanted so badly without really knowing why.

"I entered my spider in the Charleston County Middle School Science Fair."

Then she had to sit through the longest pause ever.

"And?" her father finally asked.

She couldn't help but smile.

"She won first place."

A moment ago, her father had been a scared and panicked and crazy-haired mess. But he smiled and hugged her again, dirty scrubs and all.

"First place? My baby girl? You won *first place*? Why didn't you tell me, Theresa? I would have wanted to see you win!"

"Daddy," she said, "would you really have let me go? With a tropical storm on the way? I'm surprised you're not driving us to a hotel in Georgia right now."

He shook his head and closed his eyes.

"You're right. Of course you're right. But you *should not* have snuck out like that. I'm the grown-up in this household, you know."

Theresa tried not to laugh.

"I am!"

"Okay, Dad. *You're* the grown-up."

Another pause. But this one was good. She could feel his pride for her growing.

"So can I see the ribbon or the trophy or whatever it is my brilliant daughter got for disobeying me?"

She removed the blue ribbon from her backpack. It was as

big as her head. He held it up like it was the most magnificent thing in the world.

"*First place.* My baby girl."

Now was the hard part.

"Daddy," she said. "First place—and second and third, actually—comes with an incredible, amazing, once-in-a-lifetime offer. It would be ridiculous for me to refuse."

Lightning flashed, thunder rumbled, and her father squeezed his eyes shut.

"Do I want to know what this offer entails?" he asked.

"I don't think you do," she whispered.

He shook his head, trying so hard to be the grown-up.

"You just had to win, didn't you?"

"Yeah," she said smugly. "I really had to."

CHAPTER FOUR
GIFTED

The next two and a half weeks at James Island Middle were exhausting. Theresa had always been an introvert, so to have to answer so many questions from classmates about what her summer at Flax Industries might be like really wore her out.

"Will you learn all of Dr. Flax's secrets?" "What are you going to invent?" "Will you be his best friend?" "Will you be rich?" "Can you take photos?" "Will you be in eighth grade next year or will you go straight to college?" "Will you skip college and go straight to working for Flax Industries?"

And the weirdest question of all: "Are you gifted?"

Theresa had never thought of herself as gifted or even all that smart. She simply loved goofing around with motors and welding scrap metal and bringing the mechanical creatures in her imagination to life. She never thought of building robots as work or even science—just play.

In fact, she had begun to wonder if maybe she played with robots *too* much.

She had been friends with Kayla, Tameka, and Darby since kindergarten, and they had always liked to play together. Until this year. All three of the other girls had made the James Island Middle School soccer team last January. Kayla played center back while Tameka and Darby were alternating goalies. They practiced together after school, they played games twice a week including Saturdays, and the three of them talked about soccer *all the time*. They talked about who out-skilled whom and which schools they could beat and whether they might go to the Charleston County middle school soccer championship next year.

Boring.

Soccer was a game where you tried to kick a ball to one end of the field while the other team tried to kick it to the other end. That was it. There was nothing else to it. How could they possibly talk about such an absurd game all day every day?

But her three friends since kindergarten could and did.

What Theresa liked to do after school was to weld pieces of aluminum scrap together at her uncle Robert's auto repair shop. She would buy toy robot kits that included servomotors, premanufactured parts, and instructions that told you how to create the robot on the cover of the box. But she always wanted her robots to be bigger and better, so she would replace the legs and arms of the robots with her own welded creations.

She carried these robots in progress in her backpack and

tinkered with them at lunch. Kayla, Tameka, and Darby still sat next to her in the cafeteria, and the four of them still sang along to Disney musicals that they played on their phones. They still drew on one another's book covers and pooled their spare change for doughnuts from the vending machine. But no matter what, their conversation would inevitably turn to soccer, and when it did, Theresa would grow quiet, tinkering on her robots with her head down.

That was all fine. She might have felt left out sometimes, but they were still her friends.

But once kids found out that she had won the Charleston County Middle School Science Fair and that she was going to be an inventor at Flax Industries, something changed. Suddenly, she was different.

She was the smart one.

She was the oddball.

She was *gifted*, and the word felt nothing like a compliment.

When she got a B on her final exam in social studies, she wasn't surprised. But Tameka was.

"You got a B? I thought you were gifted!"

Theresa didn't think Tameka was trying to be mean. She was just shocked.

It was a relief when the year ended. She didn't know what awaited her at Flax Industries, but it would be a welcome change from being the oddball of James Island Middle. She was excited to get to know Jon and Ashley. They seemed to like to make things the same way she did. For two and a half

weeks, she had been having imaginary conversations with them and so she already liked them, even if Ashley seemed a little bit arrogant.

But what if they didn't like *her*?

This very prospect kept her up the night before the first day of her internship. She was as anxious as she was excited. She could hear her father downstairs in his bedroom talking to himself. He was anxious, too.

Because it was so late and her mind was running in circles so fast, she wondered if she was dreaming when she heard a light, persistent tapping on her bedroom window.

She ignored it the first three times.

But then came the *tap-tap-tap* a fourth time. It was real.

She tiptoed to the window but immediately jumped back.

There was a boy outside standing on the top rung of a ladder.

He kept tapping the glass with his finger. She stood to the side of the window so she could get a closer look without letting the boy see her.

"Theresa! First-place winner Theresa Brown! *I need your help. I must* get into Flax Industries. You're my only hope. Please!"

It was a hot and humid June night, and yet the boy was wearing a puffy black winter coat with his hood on and a scarf covering most of his face. His eyes shone a brilliant and unnatural blue. Really, wrapped up the way he was, his eyes were the only part of his body she could see. When she approached the window to get a better look, he plastered himself against the glass, nearly losing his balance.

"My name is Thomas Edison, and I beg you to listen. Dr. Flax doesn't realize it, but one of his inventions is an enormous threat to this planet, and I *must* destroy it. I know that once you're inside, you'll be able to smuggle me in without his knowing."

Theresa stood there staring at his blue eyes, almost hypnotized by them. She thought she must be dreaming until the crack under her bedroom door lit up, letting her know her father had turned on the hall light.

"Theresa? Are you okay? Why are you still awake?"

He was calling to her from the bottom of the stairs.

"I'm fine, Dad!"

She knew how he was. If he sensed anything resembling a threat to her safety, he wouldn't let her go to Flax Industries in the morning.

The boy tapped the glass again, furiously without stopping. But this time, Theresa turned to face the window and put her nose up to his.

"You should know it's very dangerous to be knocking on a stranger's bedroom window in the middle of the night, Thomas Edison!"

The boy in winter clothes shook his head desperately.

"We *aren't* strangers. I introduced myself, and I already know you are the quite famous first-place spider builder Theresa Brown."

Theresa did not feel comforted or famous by this explanation.

"If you want to get into the laboratory, why don't you go ask Dr. Flax yourself? If you think one of his inventions needs to be destroyed, why don't *you* tell him?"

The boy paused, as if calculating how much he could say.

"Because even if I thought he'd believe me, my sister would be in grave danger if I said anything of the sort."

"Your sister?" Theresa gasped.

"I can't say any more," he said nervously through the glass. "And you can't tell anyone I was here, either. That would be just as bad."

"Well," she said, "you're not making a very convincing argument!"

"Theresa? What are you doing?" her father said, knocking on her bedroom door.

Theresa waved desperately at Thomas to leave.

"You have to get out of here! Now! GO!"

"Please, Theresa," he said one last time before descending the ladder. "When the opportunity comes, please let me into the laboratory. The safety of the planet depends on it."

"Theresa?" her father asked one more time. "Who are you talking to?"

"Myself," she answered. "I'm counting the stars. I'm too anxious to sleep."

Her father sighed.

"Me too."

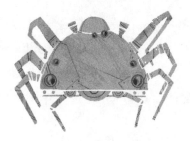

CHAPTER FIVE

WHAT'S HE BUILDING IN THERE?

Theresa could remember when the Paper Mill Mall was a bustling, thriving shopping center. She used to go there all the time with her dad. They would shop for new clothes for the coming school year, get lunch at the food court, and maybe, if she could talk him into it, buy a new robot kit from one of the three toy stores. She even met Santa Claus there. Theresa remembered wondering how the man responsible for delivering toys to all the children on the planet had the time to sit on a red-and-gold throne in a mall in Charleston, South Carolina, for the whole month of December.

But one by one, the stores had closed for one reason or another. When half of them were gone, the mall became a sad and lonely place to spend a Saturday afternoon. Then a new and larger shopping center had opened in North Charleston, which was a lot more fun and which caused even more of the old stores to close, which made the Paper Mill Mall even sadder and lonelier. Finally, the Paper Mill Mall closed altogether.

But then, after the Bionic Baby Bottom Buffer became the invention that every household with a baby had to have, Dr. Flax made a fortune and, to everyone's surprise, he bought the place. *The whole mall.*

"Can you believe it?" she remembered her father saying when he read the news on his phone. "This big-time inventor bought the whole dang thing! What in the world do you think he'll do with it?"

Everyone she knew wondered, but no one she knew had ever been inside.

Theresa felt an excitement bigger than winning first place when she saw the gray roadside sign that used to point the way to THE PAPER MILL MALL had been replaced with a larger green-and-silver sign that now read FLAX INDUSTRIES.

"Do you think his laboratory takes up the entire mall?"

"That's what they say," her father grumbled under his breath as he stopped at a red light.

She had so many more questions, especially after last night's incident with Thomas Edison. Who did that kid think he was anyway? Was he an obsessed fan of Dr. Flax's? Who lets their son run around at night with a ladder? And who names their kid *Thomas Edison*?

The light turned green, but her father didn't go. He only sat there shaking his head. He couldn't say a word, but she knew what he was thinking.

It had just been him and her for the last nine years. She knew him better than he knew himself.

"It's going to be fine, Dad. I can leave at any time. If it gets too dangerous, I mean."

He looked at her with surprise. "How would you even know, Theresa? What's he building in there? We have no idea! What if he's creating an army of giant robots with razors for teeth and guns for arms?"

"I can handle robots," she said with a sly grin.

"What if he's mixing chemicals he shouldn't be? What if you inhale toxic fumes? What if the whole place—*God forbid*—blows up?"

He was panicking again. She understood why, but his anxiety could be frustrating. She sometimes wondered, if he had *his* way, would he keep her locked in her bedroom for the rest of her life?

"If he doesn't provide us gas masks for the chemistry lessons, I'll leave. If a killer robot tries to decapitate me, I'll leave. Dad, look at it like a free summer camp. We've got nothing to lose!"

"Theresa. Baby girl. I don't *care* that it's free. I'm worried about *you*."

"I know, Dad. But Dr. Flax is giving us the opportunity to build the inventions of our dreams, and maybe—*maybe*—my

new-and-improved spider will become a Flax Industries product. What if in the future, everyone is driving a solar-powered spider? *My* spider. Can you imagine? When will I ever get a chance like this again?"

He gripped the steering wheel tightly and looked at her.

"You know," he said quietly, "sometimes, when you get so determined like this, you have your mother's voice."

"And also," she continued, "I need to know if he can do it. And if he can do it, I want to be a part of it."

Her father looked at her quizzically until the car behind them honked for them to go.

"Do what?" he asked, slowly driving forward.

"I need to know if Dr. Flax can really stop a hurricane."

He didn't respond. That was good. She had put a halt to his panic—for now.

He turned onto the exit with the sign pointing to FLAX INDUSTRIES. They drove another mile, and she felt her heart beating in her chest. But something didn't seem right. When she looked left and right, she saw nothing familiar. Had they gone the wrong way somehow? Where were all the parking lots? Were they even still in the city?

Where there had once been a vast stretch of blanched asphalt were now fields of pineapple plants. The spiky green leaves surrounded the entire former mall. Buds of fruits were beginning to show, and brilliant dragonflies flew among the leaves. Theresa knew they still had to be in the middle of downtown Charleston, but she felt more like she had been

magically transported to a tropical island where the air was clean and sweet.

Palmetto trees lined the narrow strip of dirt road that was not much wider than their car. It curved and wandered through the rows of pineapple plants as if it had never intended to lead them anywhere until, at long last, the little road brought them to the grand front entrance.

The doors were familiar. They were still the two-story-tall grand arched doors that had once opened into a luxurious shopping center. But now, instead of transparent glass, the doors were made of solid metal, and the sign above them read FLAX INDUSTRIES.

The letters of the sign were familiar, too. They were mismatched, all different fonts and sizes. Theresa recognized them from stores she used to know, recycled from signs that had once hung inside. The *F* was from Fourth Down (a sports memorabilia store), and the *LA* had been borrowed from L.A. Style (a fancy jewelry and accessory shop for fancy ladies). The *X* was from X-Treme Boards, the store where all the skater kids shopped. The other letters had been taken from restaurants, electronics stores, and coffee shops no longer housed in this once-lavish mall.

There was only a very small square of asphalt left to park their car. They pulled up alongside the only other vehicle there—a black SUV with tinted windows.

Ashley and her parents were standing in front of it, waiting patiently.

31

Ashley was dressed in a brilliant-blue dress with small pink polka dots. She was also wearing a very strong perfume that smelled like the gardenias in Theresa's backyard when they bloomed in the spring. Theresa wasn't wearing perfume. She didn't even own any. She had on an old *Frozen* T-shirt and blue jean shorts, expecting to get dirty as Dr. Flax had warned them.

Ashley's parents were dressed as if they were about to give a presentation to a corporate finance committee. In fact, they *were* going to give a presentation to a corporate finance committee later that morning. Ashley's parents were both lawyers and as serious about their work as they were about their daughter's academic success.

When she and her father got out of their car, Theresa saw that Ashley was holding the handle of a wagon containing three different aquariums, which were home to three different species of algae.

Theresa was suddenly embarrassed.

"I didn't bring my spider," she whispered to her dad. "I didn't know I was supposed to."

Her father patted her on the back. He opened the trunk, and there was her spider, folded up neatly.

"I wouldn't let you spend the summer anywhere without your secret weapon," he said.

"*You're* my secret weapon," she said quietly, and hugged him right there.

Then they took their place next to the Deans to patiently wait.

Being a friendly hospital nurse, George Brown couldn't stand next to someone for very long without saying something to break the ice.

"So! Pretty impressive work by our daughters, eh? My name's George Brown," he said, sticking out his hand to Ashley's dad.

Mr. Dean shook his hand firmly and professionally.

"Rutledge Dean. Ashley didn't take first place, but yes, impressive work," Mr. Dean agreed.

"She tried her best," her mother said flatly.

Ashley looked down at her feet.

One minute before nine, a large passenger van came careering down the palmetto-lined road, and even from a distance, they could hear voices yelling. The boisterous family-mobile came to an abrupt halt right next to them, and the side door flew open. Eight siblings bounced around inside, singing, laughing, and grabbing one another's shirts while one tried to blow his nose into his brother's sleeve.

Jon Cooper jumped out carrying a backpack and a beautifully polished, hollowed-out wooden tube with small openings carved in it from top to bottom. When he stood it up on its end, it towered three feet over him.

His mother was driving but rolled down the passenger side window to shout over the ruckus of her children.

"How y'all doing? We got ourselves some real winners here, don't we?"

"They're sure something, aren't they?" George Brown replied with a friendly wave. Ashley's parents only stared, completely stunned.

"Yeah, real great Jon gets to spend the summer here for free!" Mrs. Cooper said. "His dad and I really appreciate that. Jon's always been the scientific one. I gotta drop all his brothers and sisters off at camps this morning. Bobby Jr. here goes to basketball camp; Charlie Ann's got marching band; the twins, Rhett and Brett, are both soccer; Florence has a Girl Scouts retreat; Jackson is in a creative writing workshop for three weeks; and handsome Joey here is in Young Southern Leaders. My kids are a busy bunch!"

"I'm the youngest and the smartest," Jon said proudly as Charlie Ann leaned out the door with her trumpet and blurted three notes in his face completely off-key.

"Charlie Ann! You'll bust your brother's eardrums! Well, gotta go. You little inventors have fun, now. Congratulations to you on first place there, Miss Theresa."

Theresa smiled at the unexpected compliment while Ashley dug her toes into the gravel.

Mrs. Cooper was already turning around as Bobby Jr. reminded Jon not to be a dweeb as he pulled the van's door shut.

The Deans regarded Jon quietly. He was grinning from ear to ear.

"Y'all want to see how my new bubble maker works?"

"Sure," Theresa and her father said.

Jon was happy to oblige. He turned on a portable fan that was at the base of the vertical log, and in a few moments, enormous oval bubbles slid out of the top and bumped into one another, forming themselves into giant floating sunny-side up eggs that drifted over the pineapple plants. Then, with a cigarette lighter that a twelve-year-old boy should *not* have in his pocket, Jon lit several cups of colored incense inset vertically up the tube. In moments, the yolks of the sunny-side up eggs were filled with pink and blue and yellow smoke. On such a quiet summer morning, they looked like blobs of wild magic floating away into the Charleston sky.

"*They're beautiful.*" Theresa sighed.

"I know," Jon said proudly. "They're my best bubbles yet."

Mr. Dean was not amused.

"It's ten after nine," he said crossly, looking at his expensive watch. "Where is this famous Neil Flax?"

"He's quite often late," said a small voice behind Theresa.

Everyone jumped.

Theresa couldn't believe it.

It was *him*.

He was dressed in the same puffy winter coat with matching scarf, gloves, and boots so that only his electric-blue eyes could be seen.

"My name is Thomas Edison. It's a pleasure to meet you all."

CHAPTER SIX
NO TIME FOR TOMFOOLERY

T homas Edison shook everyone's hand, and for such a small boy, he had a *very* strong grip.

"Did you win a science fair, too?" Ashley asked him.

"*You* didn't win," Ashley's mother corrected her. "*You* came in second. Maybe this little boy won first place in another county."

Ashley looked away. Theresa turned to say something nice to her to soften her mother's blow. She also wanted to pretend like Thomas Edison wasn't there. But he stuck out his hand, and there was nothing Theresa could do but be polite, take his hand, and shake it.

The boy pulled her hand toward him quickly, forcing her down to his eye level.

"*Please* help me get inside, Theresa," he whispered urgently, but she didn't answer and tried desperately to pull away. If her father thought something weird was going on, he might panic, put her in the car, and end her internship with Dr. Flax right then and there.

"Nice to meet you" was all she said to Thomas.

She pulled and pulled, but he shook her hand again and again until her arm felt like rubber.

"Okay, that's enough now," her father said, prying her hand away from this strange boy in winter clothes. Then, finally, the front doors of the laboratory slid open and a woman moved very quickly in their direction.

Whoever she was, she had to be riding on a hoverboard, Theresa thought, because she glided toward them so incredibly fast, she could not possibly be moving on human feet.

She circled around the group before coming to an abrupt halt.

She was all business. She wore a long white laboratory coat over a dark-blue blouse buttoned up to her neck with an even darker skirt that went all the way to the ground so you couldn't even see if she was wearing shoes. Her hair seemed to be a metallic silver—if that were possible—tied sharply in the back. In her ear was the tiniest white wireless earpiece. Theresa thought she must be pretty important.

She tapped rapidly on a clipboard with a pen and scrutinized each of the three children.

"Social convention requires me to introduce myself. My name is Miss Marie Curie. I am the director of laboratory operations here at Flax Industries."

Mr. Dean perked up, at once impressed.

"Ah! Perhaps you're descended from the famous Marie Curie, the great scientist who discovered radium and the first woman to win a Nobel Prize!"

Miss Curie spun to face him, twirling around in one fluid motion.

"I am descended from no one," she snapped, and Mr. Dean didn't know what to say.

She turned back to the children and began scribbling on her clipboard.

"You're Jon Cooper. Third place."

Jon smiled and put one finger up. "You can call me Buzz."

Marie Curie was instantly perplexed.

"What? Why?"

"Because that's my name." He shrugged.

Miss Curie double-checked her clipboard.

"Buzz is not your name, you impudent little boy."

"It could be my professional nickname. Buzz the Bubble Maker!"

"No. No one gets nicknames," she said curtly and moved on.

Ashley stood up as straight as she could as Miss Curie examined her and her wagon of algae, all the while furiously tapping her pen.

"Ashley Dean. Second place."

Ashley bowed slightly and nodded. Miss Curie dashed down a note, which Ashley tried to read. Miss Curie raised her clipboard so she could not.

She moved on to Theresa and stared at her for a very long time, which made Theresa feel as awkward as ever.

"Theresa Brown. First place. Did you bring your spider?"

Thank goodness her father had thought to. Theresa pointed to it. Miss Curie noted this and then resumed staring at her.

"You seem nervous," she said.

Theresa felt exposed. "I'm not nervous."

"You are," Miss Curie said matter-of-factly, "and we have no time for confidence building. That goes for all of you. During your time spent at Flax Industries, there will be no hugs, no hand-holding, no treats if you behave, no punishments if you misbehave. You will simply be sent home if you are out of order in any way. We are in the business of building inventions that will save this planet, so we have no time for tomfoolery, nonsense, ballyhoo, goofing up, goofing off, or goofing around. Is that understood? Because I, for one, was reluctant to approve your invitations at all. Children are destructive, insolent, and easily distracted. But the good doctor insisted—Wait a minute. Step forward, young man."

Thomas Edison had been trying to hide as best he could behind Theresa, but even though he was small, he couldn't completely escape notice.

"Hello," Thomas said, trying to make his voice sound

deeper as he spoke through his winter scarf. "My name is Jon Cooper."

"No, it isn't!" the assistant said angrily, pointing at the real Jon. "*His* name is Jon Cooper."

"No, my name is Buzz," Jon said proudly.

"What did I say about tomfoolery?" she snapped.

"You said you have no time for it," Ashley said smugly. Miss Curie spun around and glided right up to her, nose to nose.

"We will have no sycophantic snobbery, either," she hissed.

Ashley's mother gave her a swat on the shoulder. "Ashley! Speak when spoken to!"

Miss Curie turned back to Thomas, who was trying to retreat into his puffy coat. Miss Curie leaned in close to him as he tried to back away.

"So. Do you still claim to be Jon Cooper, third-place winner of the Charleston County Middle School Science Fair?"

Thomas Edison processed the question for quite some time before growling in a deep, Batman-like voice, "Yes."

Miss Curie whirled around without seeming to move her feet and pulled a long needle attached to a syringe from her laboratory-coat pocket and held it up for everyone to see.

"Then you won't mind a quick blood test to prove it!"

Everyone, including Thomas Edison, gasped in horror.

"You can't take blood samples from unwilling children," Theresa's father protested. "That's illegal!"

Miss Curie grinned, and her green eyes glowed with an unnatural light.

"Watch me."

She lunged for Thomas and grabbed his left glove.

Thomas pulled his hand back, leaving the glove behind, and everyone could see his hand wasn't flesh at all but metal. Thomas quickly hid his artificial hand in his coat pocket, turned, and ran into the pineapple fields as fast as his tiny, bundled legs would carry him. They all watched him run until he ducked down behind a large pineapple plant and seemed to disappear.

"Run away and hide," Miss Curie yelled after him, "and don't come back!"

Miss Curie still held his little glove in her hand. She pocketed it, tucked the needle away, and smiled politely.

"Please excuse my scare tactics, but the doctor has been subject to envious and malicious enemies of late. I do hope you three won't prove to be as troublesome. First and foremost, my directive is to protect the owner of this laboratory and make certain no harm comes to him."

Theresa's father couldn't hold back.

"But you can't scare innocent children like that! It's not right!"

Miss Curie scoffed.

"That was no innocent child. That boy didn't let me take a sample of his blood because he is not human. He is a robot named Thomas Edison, constructed by the good doctor.

Unfortunately, he has been malfunctioning and has become a threat to our work here. Now, please, children, follow me so we can start the day. We are already behind schedule. Parents, you are welcome to leave. Return to retrieve your children at five o'clock."

Then, with a final twirl, she turned and glided toward the front door. Theresa, Ashley, and Jon stepped dutifully behind her, but Theresa's father and Ashley's parents remained where they were, not knowing how to react.

"Did she say that kid was a *robot*?" her father asked in disbelief.

Beginning to panic, he followed Theresa. Ashley's mother followed him, and then Ashley's father followed her.

Theresa felt her blood pumping with excitement. She had always wanted to build a robot indistinguishable from real life, and it appeared that Dr. Flax had really done it! She wondered if she could do the same. Maybe she could improve on her spider's design so that she would look like a giant twin-flagged jumping spider—the coolest of all the spiders. But she didn't say a word of this. She could tell her father was having second thoughts about letting her stay, and probably third and fourth thoughts, too.

As Miss Curie approached the large metal front doors, they slid open before her, revealing an enormous lobby. The children audibly gasped and so did their parents. Miss Curie whirled around as if she were skating on ice.

"Didn't you hear me? No parents! Children, if you want to come in, come in. Otherwise, you're free to go home."

Theresa turned to see her father anxiously stepping forward and backward. He reached out like he wanted to take his daughter's hand, drive her home, and never let her outdoors until the summer was over.

Theresa took her father's hands and spoke as gently as she could.

"Daddy, I can leave at any time. But I *have* to take this chance. I might just build something that can make this planet a better place. And if Dr. Flax can really stop hurricanes and save lives, then I know you'll be proud of me for being a part of that."

Her father stared at her, stunned.

Maybe she could give a good speech after all.

He stepped back. He exhaled.

Her father let go.

"Okay," he said. "You've got me tongue-tied, baby girl. You go get 'em."

"Thanks, Dad," she said, giving him a quick hug. "Don't worry."

But she knew he would anyway. Still, she couldn't resist what might lay beyond the doors before her, no matter how dangerous.

She turned and followed Ashley, Jon, and the peculiar Miss Curie into the laboratory.

CHAPTER SEVEN

INTO THE LABORATORY

After her first steps into the laboratory, Theresa gasped out loud.

"Whoa. I can't believe it!"

She hadn't expected the shopping mall to look as it once had, but she certainly didn't think Dr. Flax would have transformed it into *this*.

Flax Industries was like no laboratory she had seen in books or movies. This was no sterile, artificial stainless-steel environment with computer screens on every wall. There were no scientists in white coats peering into microscopes, no fluorescent lights, no polished floors. There weren't even any chairs or tables.

Instead, there was only—Theresa inhaled deeply to smell it—*life*.

Flowers blossomed in every corner. Purple wisteria bloomed on vines along the upper-story guardrail. Pink azaleas had overtaken the toddler bouncy rides. Red bougainvillea flowers covered the kiosks where sales clerks used to sell cell phone covers and perfume. White and yellow roses sprang from pots placed in every available corner.

Where there weren't flowers, there were gardens of fruits and vegetables. Well-tended rows of watermelon, tomatoes, onions, carrots, and cabbages stretched down the middle of the walkways, and lemon and lime trees marched along either side. Theresa had never been in a garden so full and lush. She nearly forgot she was indoors. She even felt the warmth of sunlight.

When she looked up, she saw that Dr. Flax had expanded the former skylights. There were more skylights than ceiling now, with solar panels in between the panes. Sparrows flew around her head, and she even heard the distant rapid hammering of a woodpecker.

Jon and Ashley were equally awestruck, looking in every direction, trying to make sense of the place. Was this really the shopping mall they had known before?

Only the enormous stone fountain remained, but now it was covered in moss and vines. Water no longer sprayed up to the ceiling, and the basin below had been transformed from a clear pool where customers once tossed coins into a dark-green pond full of lily pads, frogs, and algae. There was even a duck missing an eye paddling happily in a circle.

Two escalators still crisscrossed behind the fountain, but they were no longer running. One of them had been rebuilt

into a ramp. Ivies with green leaves and small white flowers curled around and up the handrails.

And surrounding them on all sides was the sound of rushing water.

"Is there a waterfall in here?" Theresa asked Miss Curie with wonder.

"Yes, Miss Brown. The good doctor has filled the walls and the floor below with pipes of water that are constantly moving. This brilliant design cools the building in the summer and captures heat during the winter. The water moves through so many natural purifiers, you can open any of the taps you see in the walls to get a refreshing drink of the cleanest water you've ever tasted."

Jon immediately ran to the nearest tap, put his mouth under it, and turned it on so that water poured all over his face.

"She's right! This water is crystal clear and ice-cold!"

"You're embarrassing yourself," Ashley scolded, but Jon kept on drinking.

Ashley knelt at the fountain's basin to admire all the different species of algae there.

"These specimens are so beautiful," she said. "I love how bright and red they are."

Miss Curie tapped her pen on her clipboard impatiently. "Yes, yes. The doctor is quite an accomplished phycologist. We house two hundred and sixteen different types of red algae here, all of which are edible."

Ashley perked up.

"Dr. Flax collects algae? I can't wait to show him mine in more detail!"

Miss Curie smirked at her condescendingly. "Your species of blue-green pond scum is hardly unique, Miss Dean. Your second-place spirulina is commonplace and frequently found off the coast of the Florida Keys. I imagine you collected yours while on vacation with your arrogant parents."

Jon started laughing, spitting out a mouthful of water.

Ashley turned away, crushed.

Theresa couldn't understand why Miss Curie had to be so mean. Her father had taught her that it was rude to use such insulting words like *arrogant*, especially when applied to people you had just met.

She stepped up to Ashley carefully.

"I bet Dr. Flax hasn't made spirulina tortillas like yours, though. It's one thing to collect algae, but it takes talent to make them into real food. I think your tortillas taste as good as any I've ever had. You're a very good chef."

Ashley turned angrily on her. "I'm a *phycologist*, not a *chef*."

"We have an assortment of condiments available in our entirely vegan kitchen if you would like to add a bit more flavor to your algae dishes so that they are tolerable."

Theresa jumped at the voice.

Standing right behind her was a young man with piercing golden eyes and black hair gelled and sharply parted. He was wearing a dark-blue suit with an even darker tie, plus an

unusual faux-leather apron with the imprint of a pineapple on the front. FLAX was stamped across the top of it, and a whole assortment of tools stuck out of the pockets. He didn't seem to care that he had startled Theresa. He bent down with his hands behind his back to study her spider.

"This machine could prove useful," he said, but he didn't explain any further. He looked briefly into Ashley's aquariums but didn't acknowledge Ashley herself, who stood up a little straighter, eager to answer any questions he might have. Then the young man took a look at Jon's bubble maker.

"Why the obsession with bubbles?" he sneered.

Jon shrugged. "I don't know. I just love them. They're perfect spheres formed in nature for one thing. Why do you put so much gel in your hair? It makes you look like you're made of plastic."

"Why are you so rude?" the man snapped back.

"Are you an inventor here, too?" Theresa asked.

"He's not an inventor of anything," Miss Curie answered before he could.

The young gentleman gave her a menacing look and straightened his tie and apron.

"My name is Zachary Flax. I'm the doctor's nephew and protégé."

"You're not anyone's protégé, either," Miss Curie said, impatient as ever. "Where *is* Dr. Flax? Is he all right? He hasn't texted me all morning! He left without telling me where he was

going again. We can't afford to have another accident on the premises. Dr. Flax's safety is paramount!"

"I'm quite all right, Marie. You need not fret, although I always appreciate your concern for my welfare."

They all turned to see Dr. Flax walking briskly toward them from the eastern end of the laboratory. He was once again wearing boots covered in black pluff mud and carrying what looked like a fencing mask with electronic enhancements.

Miss Curie immediately started flying around the doctor like Mercury in orbit, hot and fast and buzzing with questions.

"How good to see you, Doctor. Are you okay? Will you be going out again this morning? Can I send these children home? They really are dangerous little creatures. They will only impede my ability to protect you."

Dangerous little creatures? Theresa didn't want to be perceived like that or be a guest in a laboratory where she wasn't wanted. Her father certainly wouldn't mind if she turned around and walked home right now. Ashley perked right up and pretended like Marie Curie hadn't said a word.

"It's a real honor to be here, Dr. Flax," she said. "I've always been the best student in my class, so I know I'll be the best student here, as well."

Jon rolled his eyes clear to the ceiling.

But Dr. Flax grinned and bowed quite formally before them all.

"No, Miss Dean, it is indeed *my* honor to have the three of

you here. We are going to accomplish so much this summer. And, Marie, you need not worry your little robot head about these young scientists causing any trouble—you're doing an excellent job fulfilling your programming."

Marie Curie is a robot, too?

"No way!" Jon shouted.

Miss Curie seemed rather embarrassed by the comment. She stopped tapping her pen and circling the doctor. When she came to a halt, her skirt fluttered just enough for Theresa to see that Miss Curie's ankles did not end in shoes or even feet but a single silver ball. Theresa tried not to stare—she didn't want to be rude. But Miss Curie was a robot!

"Do you like your laboratories?" the doctor asked enthusiastically. "I ordered the furnishings specifically for each of you."

What? Her own personal laboratory? Theresa exchanged excited looks with Jon and even Ashley.

"I have yet to show them their labs, Uncle Neil," Zachary said wearily. He seemed like a man desperately in need of a nap.

Miss Curie started tapping her pen again. "That's *Dr. Uncle Neil* to you, Zach."

Zachary pushed her on the forehead with two fingers, causing her to roll backward.

"*Dr. Uncle* is not proper English, Marie. Maybe you're malfunctioning, just like poor Thomas."

"Zachary, Marie, *please*," the doctor said, as if he had heard

these two bicker too many times before. "Let us be courteous in front of our guests. Yes, my new friends, you will each have a laboratory of your own equipped with everything you need to let your imaginations soar! Perhaps you will even build something worthy of being included in next year's Flax Inventions for a Better World catalog."

Ashley side-eyed Theresa for a split second, but Theresa knew that look well enough from every competitive kid she had ever encountered in school. The I'm-going-to-crush-you-and-let-you-know-it look. But Theresa didn't want to crush anyone. Weren't they on the same team?

"Each day you'll arrive at nine," Dr. Flax continued. "Please eat a good breakfast before your arrival because you'll promptly begin working in your laboratories. The morning has been scientifically proven to be the most productive time of day, so I want you three to have that time to yourselves to learn, to explore, to create. Then at noon, my nephew will provide you a delicious and healthy salad he's made himself. Salad construction really is his greatest talent."

At this compliment, Zachary let out the longest rumbling groan she had ever heard. It was really quite uncalled for and seemed like a sound a disobedient child would make. But the doctor ignored it as if this, too, was a frequent occurrence.

"After lunch, we will have a group discussion about environmental science that will hopefully prove useful to all of us. After that, there will be more time to work in your laboratories. Then at five o'clock, you'll return home, where I hope

you'll get a good night's rest—a lot can be accomplished while dreaming, you know. Does that schedule suit everyone?"

The schedule suited Theresa just fine. She couldn't believe her luck! Mornings of pure unsupervised inventing and afternoon discussions with the great Dr. Flax? What could be better?

"So, Zachary, if you will kindly show our new colleagues to their laboratories, I must resume my search for the lost member of our family. Our sweet Tommy has gotten some bad ideas in his head and is hiding himself from us. But have no fear, I've invented just the tool to find him!"

Dr. Flax raised the futuristic fencing mask. He also removed a pair of golden gloves from one of his many overall pockets.

"This Sensory Amplifier has proven useful on more than one occasion. It will enhance my vision one hundred times. My hearing will be amplified as much as I can bear. These gloves will allow me to sense movement when I put my hands in the mud or the water, and even my sense of smell will be heightened, although I'm not certain Tommy has any discernible odor."

"What about taste?" Jon asked.

"Well, the Amplifier does not increase the potency of the human taste buds at present, and I'm not sure what I could taste that would lead me to one undoubtedly very lonely and confused robot. But for a future model, your suggestion is a good one, Mr. Cooper."

"Is this hunt really necessary?" Marie Curie said anxiously.

"Thomas is probably gone for good. Maybe we should accept that he's had an unfortunate fate—"

"But we all saw him this morning," Ashley interrupted. "You almost stuck him with a needle, and then he ran off into the pineapple fields."

Miss Curie whipped around on her rolling ball with murder in her electric eyes.

"Why don't you keep your smug little mouth shut, Miss Dean?"

"Yes, Miss Dean," Zachary agreed haughtily. "You are quite out of order."

"*What?*" Dr. Flax gasped, completely taken aback. "Can this be true, Marie? Why wouldn't you have informed me immediately? I've been searching the marsh since sunrise, and you knew he was in our front yard all this time? I simply don't understand your resentment toward your own brother. I never programmed you with the emotion of jealousy, and yet you exhibit all the qualities of an envious and spiteful younger sibling. If valuable time wasn't being lost, I'm afraid we'd have to have a serious examination of your central processing unit!"

So it was Marie who Thomas considered a sister! She was the one Thomas had expressed such concern for last night. And yet, she had chased him away this morning and told him never to come back.

Miss Curie, if it was possible for a robot, looked embarrassed

and tried to avoid eye contact with the doctor. But he took her hands in his and held them tight.

"Marie, you will be joining me in the pineapple fields. Perhaps this will be the morning that we can reunite my children and iron out any grievances you two may have. Then, finally, I can get back to my special project."

Dr. Flax turned to Theresa, Ashley, and Jon.

"My apologies, friends. Let's not allow this family spat to delay you three. Zachary, if you please, show them to their laboratories. I can't wait to hear what you all think of them."

"Yes, Uncle." Zachary sighed, already exhausted by the task. As he walked up the ramp, waving for them to follow, Jon whispered excitedly to Theresa.

"Isn't this crazy? I bet Dr. Flax and his nephew are robots, too!"

She would have never thought such a thing, but now Theresa really did wonder.

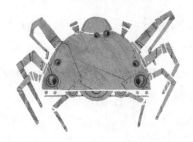

CHAPTER EIGHT
PERSONAL LABORATORIES

Zachary led them up the ivy-covered ramp to the upper level of the western wing of the mall where, he said with utmost boredom, they would find their personal laboratories.

He didn't offer to carry Theresa's spider or pull Ashley's wagon full of algae or lug Jon's six-foot-tall wooden bubble maker. Theresa didn't mind carrying her spider, but it would have only been proper Southern manners for their host to have at least offered.

As they walked, Zachary pointed out the different rooms and their intended purposes. Each room, once a former store, was locked with a solid metal gate pulled down from the ceiling. Above each gate was the room's new name spelled out, like the sign above the front doors, in a mismatch of letters recycled from the stores that used to occupy the Paper Mill Mall.

Zachary walked slowly, as if to deliberately dull their excitement.

"To our left is PLASTICS. You'll see three large bins by its gate. If you have any plastic refuse at home that can't be recycled, please bring it tomorrow. We go through twenty bins a day, and we can always use more."

"You need *unrecyclable* plastic? What for?" Ashley asked curiously.

"The thing inside eats it," Zachary replied. "It is *always* hungry."

Jon put his ear up to the metal gate. "There's something growling in there."

"You should know it also devours children. Let's keep moving."

Theresa wanted to take a listen, too, but she also didn't want to miss anything. She couldn't wait to see her laboratory. She wondered which of the former stores it would be. The shoe store, Ten East? One of the pet stores? The goofy souvenir shop, Dexter's? There were so many possibilities.

As they walked, Theresa marveled at how much Nature thrived inside the laboratory. Every former store was now surrounded by trees, flowers, and bushes. Everywhere were birds, squirrels, and even bees. There was no longer need for electric lighting—sunlight poured in through the skylights. There was no longer need for soft ambient shopping music—the calming rush of water surrounded them. It was as if Nature and technology had finally learned how to live together in harmony, even if only in this building.

"This room is for the drones," Zachary said, waving to his

left casually without stopping. Sure enough, in unlit neon letters taken from old food court restaurants, the room was aptly labeled DRONES.

Again, Jon put his ear to the gate.

"I hear them!"

Ashley and Theresa couldn't resist pressing their ears to the metal. Theresa did hear a buzzing that grew louder, then receded, then grew louder again, as if the drones inside were flying in circles.

"Of course you hear them," Zachary said. "They're always flying. We don't turn them off. We *can't* turn them off. *Never* go in this room. The awful things have caused too many accidents in the laboratory already."

Each room was locked with a padlock. Theresa had never seen locks so large. Instead of simple and small keypads, they were large, glowing color wheels the size of pizzas. They were set into the right side of each gate. The locks reminded her of her old electronic memory game Simon, except these discs were comprised of thirteen wedges instead of four. The wedges were red, orange, yellow, green, blue, purple, and shades in between.

On closer examination, she saw that each wedge was labeled with an animal and its silhouette. Born and raised in South Carolina, Theresa immediately recognized that all the animals were native to her state. There was an American alligator (scary), a red-tailed hawk, a blue crab, a loggerhead sea turtle (she'd seen baby loggerheads in real life scurrying to find the ocean by moonlight), a great egret (the prettiest

one), a copperhead snake (scarier), a bobcat, a redfish (her dad's favorite), a Boykin Spaniel (*her* favorite), a blacktip shark (the scariest!), a bottlenose dolphin (supersmart and friendly), a pig frog (cute), and the cannonball jellyfish, many of which she had seen washed up on Folly Beach.

It was really the coolest lock she had ever seen, and she wanted to start pressing the wedges. She wondered why anyone would make a keypad lock so tempting. But then she had to ask herself why most locks were so boring. If you must have a lock on your door, why not make it as colorful and creative as this one?

"And here we have Jon's laboratory."

All three children gasped out loud. His name had been spelled out in three large letters above the entrance: JON. Theresa recognized the oversize *J* that had been borrowed from one of the department stores—J. M. Quarter's.

Jon laughed with delight and ran inside.

"It's a bubble maker's paradise!"

His lab had once been a Cindi's Cinnamon Buns. The ovens, chairs, and goofy pink-and-white decorations had been removed, but the large counters and sinks remained. There was all the space a master bubble maker could want. In addition, Dr. Flax had provided Jon a wide assortment of tools and equipment to allow his imagination to run wild.

There were tubs of different soaps, containers of starches, and biodegradable plastic bubble-making frames of all kinds. There were air compressors, fans, helium tanks, and even a tiny

windmill sitting abreast a tiny moving river on a table covered with teeny-tiny models of houses, roads, and mountains. There were stacks of tubes to use—*lots* of tubes—wide, long, narrow, short, wavy, wiggly, and one that twisted like a pretzel.

There was also an assortment of paints, a desk with a sketch pad and pencils, and a whiteboard that interacted with a laptop computer so that, when ready, Jon could give a presentation on whatever he had invented.

"And it's mine for the whole summer?" Jon asked, almost not believing it.

"For the whole summer." Zachary sighed begrudgingly while wiping his eyes. "You'll note that there is a lock on the inside as well as the outside. I will whisper your combination in your ear."

He leaned over, cupped his hand to Jon's ear, and said it very quietly. Jon listened carefully.

"Cool," he said, grinning with delight. "That'll work."

"Of course it will work," Zachary said. "Don't forget it, because you may need to lock yourself in your lab one day."

"Why would we ever have to lock ourselves *inside*?" Ashley asked.

Zachary laughed out loud. "Because some of these inventions have not been perfected and are more prone to cause harm than good. Some of them really should be put out of their misery if you were to ask me, but"—he sighed—"no one ever does."

Theresa decided she would not tell her father about *that*.

"Let's keep moving," Zachary said to Jon. "You'll have time to play later."

Jon followed reluctantly. He clearly wanted to stay behind and see what else he could find in his bubble-making lab.

"Bubbles. Of all possible passions," Theresa heard their host mutter as they continued their walk. "Such a waste of talent."

They came to Ashley's laboratory next. ASHLEY was spelled out beautifully in cursive letters borrowed from the former candle shop, the flower shop, and Fish, Fish, Fish, the tropical fish shop that had once occupied this room.

Ashley dropped her wagon handle and put her hands to her head in disbelief.

"This is *my* laboratory? *Mine?*"

"It meets with your approval, then?" Zachary sighed.

Ashley was on the verge of tears.

"It's simply magnificent."

It really was. All three children wandered through its aisles. In many ways, this space was as Theresa remembered it when it was a fish shop—aquariums of all sizes lined the shelves. But now, instead of fish, the tanks were full of colorful algae. Where there had once been an aisle of fish food and nets, there were now bags and bags of powdered nutrients. Along the back wall, there were test tubes, Bunsen burners, and everything one would need for chemistry experiments. There were all different manners of grow lights organized by size and type, and there was even a giant clay oven where Ashley could cook

anything she wanted (even though she was a phycologist and *not* a chef).

Where there had once been a staff break room, there was now a very professional office with a desk and a whiteboard and accompanying laptop like the one in Jon's lab. There were neat piles of paper, pens, pencils, and journals for her to record and reflect on her various phycology experiments.

There was also a giant koi pond in the center of the room with a waterfall pouring into it from the ceiling. Beautiful koi of all colors swam among the lily pads that had been placed there. There were plastic dividers in the pond, too, so that Ashley could separate different species of algae there as she saw fit.

It was a beautifully constructed laboratory, and Theresa told Ashley so. She only hoped hers would be as nice.

"My parents would be so proud to see me here," Ashley said quietly to herself.

Zachary whispered her lock combination to her as well. Ashley listened very seriously and then asked him to repeat it so she was sure she had it. Zachary grumbled like he was being asked to move a boulder up a mountain, but he told it to her again.

"C'mon," he said. "Let's go to Spider Girl's room and get this over with."

They walked past several more locked storefronts that did not have names above their doors. Jon asked about them all.

"What's the deal with this one?" "What's behind this door?" "What about that one over there?"

But Zachary ignored all his inquiries. Theresa began to worry when they came to a stop at the end of the upper walkway. There was nowhere else to go. Before them was the enormous closed-down department store Belstrom's. It used to be a nice store where she and her father shopped for her school clothes every summer. Now it was closed, with a large plastic tarp hanging from the ceiling to cover both the first- and second-floor entrances.

"Well," Zachary said with a shrug. "This is it." And he pulled on a thick rope that was hanging from the scaffolding next to him.

The tarp fell to the floor with a dramatic *WHUMP!*

They all looked up in awe. In gigantic, glorious letters borrowed from the old Belstrom's sign and the fancier department store Headley's, from the eastern end of the mall, was *her* name, bigger and bolder than she had ever dared imagine it—THERESA.

Zachary pressed the animal-padlock combination, and the large metal gate that guarded her laboratory began to rise. Parakeets and chickadees flew from the lemon trees outside of it as the interior was revealed.

It was huge.

Enormous, really.

"Whoa" was all Theresa could say.

To which Jon started laughing.

"Oh man, Theresa! You got the penthouse suite!"

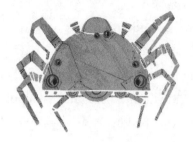

CHAPTER NINE
BEWARE THE ENVIOUS

A department store without a perfume counter or racks of clothes or kiosks filled with purses or dressing rooms or dividing walls or wandering customers seems *very* large and *very* empty and a space that any twelve-year-old scientist would instinctively want to run wild through.

That's exactly what Jon did.

He raced through Theresa's laboratory in one big circle, laughing and yelling just to hear his own voice echo.

"This is AMAAAAAAAYYYYYYYZING!" he screamed.

Theresa walked through the space slowly, as if she were stepping into a dream. She wouldn't have thought or even hoped that this could happen to her—to be given a laboratory big enough to build whatever she wanted. *Anything at all.* She put down her spider, stretched her arms out wide, and slowly spun around.

But did Dr. Flax not think she would need additional supplies? Tools and maybe some spare parts? She supposed she could bring in scrap from her uncle Robert's auto repair shop. And she didn't mind using her own portable arc welding kit. But couldn't he have at least provided her a table to work on?

But her question was soon answered when Jon ran down the escalator to the first floor.

"Hey, you guys! You've got to see this!"

Theresa followed. As she walked down to the lower level, a joy began to grow in her, a joy very much like the excitement she felt walking down the stairs many past Christmas mornings, knowing that magnificent mechanical toys had magically appeared in the night and now lay waiting for her, lovingly displayed in a semicircle on the living room floor for her to find and unwrap and tinker with all day. It was a joy big enough to let her forget about the black hole inside her—at least for a while.

As she moved off the last step of the escalator, she saw an incredible sight spread before her, and the growing joy filled her all the way up.

The entire first floor of her lab was a robot builder's paradise.

A row of brand-new torches of all sizes for soldering, brazing, and welding lay in a neat row before her. Behind them, there were 3D printing machines of all sizes, rods and sheets of aluminum, and every possible joint and hinge and hook.

There were electric lights, a variety of seats and steering wheels, and a toolbox so big, it had wheels and an engine of its own. She'd never seen such a thing—a toolbox that could be driven like a truck!

There were stacks of boxes and crates of car parts, truck parts, boat parts, Jet Ski parts, and even snowmobile parts (even though it hadn't snowed in South Carolina for five years). There were chains and nets and ropes and appliances she couldn't even identify.

There was a forklift, too, which required a license to operate—a license she didn't have. But there it was for her use anyway.

There were computers—*lots* of computers. Every kind Theresa had heard of and many she had not. Laptops and desktops, spare circuit boards, extra microprocessors, and an electronic whiteboard like Jon's and Ashley's. She could only imagine how many kinds of software were available to help her design whatever she liked.

She might have stood there all day admiring it if Zachary didn't groan from impatience.

"Let me tell you your lock combination," he said. "I have far more important things than babysitting awaiting me."

Theresa cleared her mind. She certainly didn't want to forget the combination, but she didn't want to have to ask for it twice like Ashley.

Zachary leaned down, cupped his hand to her ear, and whispered it quickly and impatiently: "Boykin Spaniel—loggerhead

sea turtle—blue crab—blue crab—blue crab—red-tailed hawk—great egret."

It was a long password, but the three blue crabs in the middle would make it easier to remember. And with her favorite dog at the beginning and a beautiful egret at the end, she knew she had it. She repeated it to herself just to make sure as she walked in circles around her laboratory.

Her laboratory.

It was so *big*. Almost too big. She made herself dizzy taking it all in.

But even while she was so ecstatic, so thrilled to have a space of her own with all the welding and designing tools she'd ever need, she couldn't ignore the guilt she felt. She could *feel* Ashley's energy behind her. She didn't dare look, but she knew Ashley was standing at the top of the escalator looking down at her, radiating envy and frustration and downright anger.

Finally, Theresa couldn't ignore her any longer. She turned around to face her.

"*It's . . . not . . . FAIR*," Ashley growled between her teeth.

"You're not satisfied with your lab?" Zachary asked with a bit of mockery.

Ashley didn't answer.

"Dr. Flax wanted you to have the very best in accommodations, Miss Dean. If you feel that you have been cheated in any way, I will consider it my duty to tell him."

Ashley remained silent. It was obvious to all of them that

Zachary would very much enjoy telling his uncle that she was not grateful for his efforts.

But Ashley would not behave so improperly.

"No," she finally said, looking down at her feet and straightening her polka-dot dress. "I like my lab very much. I will get to work right away."

Then she walked out of Theresa's laboratory and back to her own. Theresa wanted to chase after her. She almost said, *Hey, if you would like to trade laboratories, we can!*

Almost.

But she did not. Because she realized Ashley might just take her up on it.

"Someone is apparently quite jealous," Zachary said as he began to leave.

"Why?" Theresa asked. "Her lab is just as cool, even if it's not as big. Hers has tons of aquariums and algae and a big clay oven. She even has a waterfall and real live fish!"

Zachary chuckled softly.

"Some cannot stand to take second place, no matter how great their own rewards," he said. "Beware the envious, Miss Brown. They think they have to destroy your world before they can create their own."

Zachary walked slowly away, and there Theresa was with a whole laboratory to create whatever she wanted and a whole summer to do it.

She felt very anxious at that moment, suddenly realizing she was supposed to—*expected to*—do something fantastic

and world-changing and bigger than anything she had done before.

She felt very alone.

Until she realized that Jon had returned to the upper level to run in more circles.

"Echo! Echo! ECHO!" he yelled as he flew. "We are the greatest scientists in the world! No one can stop us! Flax Industries is AMAAAAAAAYYYYYYYZING!"

CHAPTER TEN
POSSIBILITY

Jon eventually went back to his lab to explore and start manufacturing even greater bubbles. Left alone, Theresa turned on one of the computers and found her favorite online music station—All Disney Musicals. The computer was attached to a pair of speakers six feet tall. She turned the volume up to eleven.

Then she danced.

While "Be Our Guest" echoed through her laboratory, she twirled around *her* computers and *her* set of welding torches and *her* 3D printers, the biggest of which took up the entire former fitting room of the girls' clothing department. She sang as loud as she wanted because this space was all hers to create *whatever* she wanted—all because of a spontaneous whim to enter a science fair.

Well, at least for the summer.

Then, less than three months from now, she would start eighth grade. She would be taking chemistry and physics, dropping eggs with parachutes and dissecting unfortunate frogs. Would eighth grade be the most anticlimactic school year ever after a summer like this? She couldn't help but think about it. Would she have to go back to playing with pocket-size robots at the lunch table while her friends talked about soccer?

As a scientist, she wondered, *Am I peaking at twelve years old? Is it all downhill from here?*

She pushed these questions out of her mind and tried to concentrate.

Dr. Flax had said she should try to create something that would make the world a better place. It was a tall order. What did he mean exactly? She knew her invention should be something that made the world a cleaner place or at least not a dirtier one—that much was obvious. And, she decided, a good invention would make life easier for people instead of harder. But what could do that?

She stopped dancing and sat on the floor in front of her spider with her knees to her chin.

She felt a peaceful calm flow through her. She really loved this spider. She was like a pet that Theresa had raised since she was a baby. In her early stages, she was nothing more than a platform of LEGOs and eight simple servomotors that controlled her legs. But from there, she had grown and grown. The LEGO platform had been replaced with an aluminum

sheet, and Theresa soon gave her legs twice their original length welded from scrap. Before long, her spider wasn't operated with a remote control but by actually sitting on her and controlling her with a steering wheel. Theresa was always tinkering with her and making her better, and with each change she made, she loved her spider that much more.

But was her spider an invention that could make the world a better place? Theresa didn't know. She was solar-powered, so at least she didn't add pollution to the air. Did she belong in next year's Flax Inventions for a Better World catalog? She didn't know that, either.

Theresa wished she was more like Ashley. Ashley was so dedicated to making the world a better place with science. Even if she was really uptight and kind of mean, at least she knew who she was and why she was doing it. You could tell right away that she had ambition. Theresa didn't doubt that Ashley would someday end starvation, because she wasn't going to let anyone tell her she couldn't. Theresa worried she didn't have that kind of drive.

But then, she also wished she was more like Jon. He liked bubbles because he liked bubbles. Simple as that. She doubted he cared what anyone else thought about him. Not caring gave him the freedom to truly be himself. Jon might make the world a better place, if making the world a better place happened to coincide with making bubbles. She doubted he cared about the Flax Inventions for a Better World catalog. He probably hadn't even read it.

Theresa really only knew one thing—she wanted to live in a world where mothers didn't drown in floods.

But if she or Dr. Flax couldn't make that happen, then second best would be to love this spider by making her better.

"But what do *you* want, girl?" she asked her spider. "Do you want to be bigger? Or faster? Do you want to jump or climb?"

Theresa held her knees to her chest, rocking back and forth, waiting for her spider to answer.

"Do you want to shoot a web?"

She caught her breath by her own question.

Of course she wanted to shoot a web! She was a spider, after all.

Theresa thought about it, her chin between her knees. Sticky ropes? No, that seemed impractical. Her spider would have to shoot a web so strong that she could pull her own weight and a rider and a passenger up a wall. That was more than one hundred pounds. To accomplish that, a spider would need . . .

Grappling hooks.

She stood up excitedly and started looking through all the supplies Dr. Flax had provided for her. There were so many boxes and crates. It was fun opening them to discover all the tools and attachments. She forgot more than once what she was looking for. But eventually, she uncovered a cardboard box packed with brand-new three-pronged hooks.

They would work perfectly.

Then, even though Dr. Flax had provided her computers

equipped with the latest design software, Theresa used pen and paper to sketch two slingshots that she would attach to two swiveling handles. The slingshots would fire the grappling hooks tethered to zip lines in any direction she liked. But was there a zip line in her laboratory? After searching for ten minutes and being frequently distracted, she found a whole roll of it.

Then she uncovered two fishing reels that she could attach to the slingshots and use to reel in the zip line after she fired the hooks. She'd be able to pull herself toward whatever the hooks had grabbed. The design had come to her quickly and easily, as her best ideas always did.

Next was the fun part—bringing her drawing to life.

She picked out a torch and a mask and was soon welding the slingshots out of the aluminum and stainless-steel rods piled neatly for her in a corner. It was almost as if Dr. Flax had anticipated all the supplies she would need to improve her spider, even before she knew what those improvements would be. Next, she got to work on the swiveling handles. She attached these to two mounts on either side of the driver's seat.

By eleven o'clock, her spider was much improved, nearly ready to shoot a web and climb walls. She was so engrossed in welding and humming Disney songs, she didn't know how long Dr. Flax had been standing behind her.

"Hello there," he finally shouted over the music and the buzz of the electric generator.

She jumped but quickly recovered when she saw it was him. She turned off her torch, lifted her welding mask, shut off the music, turned, and smiled.

"Hello," she said quietly.

Dr. Flax was wearing his excessively pocketed white overalls and his rubber wading boots and was completely drenched. His mop of white-and-black curls was a tangled mess, but he didn't acknowledge how wet he was, so neither did she.

"Hmm," he said, examining her work. "Dual grappling hooks, I see. A logical addition. A spider should be able to shoot a web and climb up a wall, shouldn't it?"

"Exactly what I was thinking," Theresa said proudly.

He smiled and paced around her work. He leaned in close to examine the swivel mounts and ran his finger along the freshly welded joints.

"Very nice craftmanship. Good fusion. No globs, no cracks."

"Thanks," she said. She knew what she was doing.

"I've just spoken to Miss Dean and Mr. Cooper. Miss Dean wants to create a whole variety of new algae foods that could be easily shipped to the most remote parts of the world. Mr. Cooper is building a bubble organ. I don't know what he means exactly, but his excitement is infectious. What's next after grappling hooks, Miss Brown?"

She thought about it.

"I don't know," she finally said.

Then there was a long, awkward pause. Theresa was quite

used to these pauses in her life—she rarely knew what to say in conversations with adults. Well, anyone really. But she didn't want to have an awkward pause with the famous Dr. Flax. He was so selfless, seeming to care only about others—like her dad. And he was so passionate about robots and creating things—like herself. He was more interested in her invention than fetching himself a towel.

He sat down on a pile of sheet metal.

"Aren't you cold?" she finally dared to ask.

He patted down his wet overalls and smiled. "I'm fine," he said. "I'm more frustrated than cold."

"Why?"

He laughed as if she had told him a good joke, even though she had no idea what that joke might be. Dr. Flax lost himself in thought for a bit, not seeming to mind that another awkward pause was inflating the space between them.

"Well," he finally said, "I have yet to find Thomas. On top of that, my latest invention continues to frustrate and confound me. And I'm all wet."

Dr. Flax ran his hand through his curly wet locks and let out a big, exasperated sigh. Maybe now was not the time to probe, but Theresa wanted to know so badly.

"May I ask you a question, Dr. Flax?"

"Of course, Miss Brown," he said quietly.

"What is your latest invention?"

"Well," he said, "it's quite ambitious. It's either my magnum opus or my greatest failure. Hard to tell at this stage.

The laws of thermodynamics can be awfully stubborn. I call it my Big Zero, and I think it's something that might really slow climate change and return balance to our planet."

"What does it do?" she asked. Then, hopefully, "*Can it stop hurricanes?*"

He smiled, shut his eyes, and clapped his hands quietly together.

"Perhaps it can stop hurricanes. If I could only get it right."

Another long silence hung between them.

"What if you can't?"

Dr. Flax shrugged.

"Then I will have failed. And not for the first time, either. But that's okay. With every failure, I learn something, Miss Brown, and learning something is always worthwhile."

He smiled again, but it seemed forced. In his eyes she saw that he was lost, sad, and tired.

"I want to protect our environment, too," she said quickly. "I wish *I* could make something like Ashley's edible algae that could end hunger. I wish I had an idea like that. That would be really cool."

"That would be cool," he agreed. "You know, Miss Brown, you should tell Miss Dean you think so. She would appreciate the compliment. She's quite intimidated by you."

What did he say? Theresa was sure that she had never intimidated *anybody* in her whole life—least of all Ashley Dean, student body president of Daniel Island Middle School.

"I don't know why," she said softly. "I'm not as smart as she is. I'm just good at tinkering with robots."

"You think too little of your solar-powered robotic spider," he said. "I see great potential for it to change this planet. For one thing, your spider leaves no carbon footprint."

"Yes," Theresa agreed. "But neither does a bicycle."

"True!" he said excitedly, clapping his hands. "And don't we owe the great Karl von Drais applause for inventing the bicycle!"

Dr. Flax wiped the wet hair out of his eyes one more time.

"But surely you've imagined a world where everyone owns a solar-powered robotic spider with dual grappling hooks? No potholes or fallen trees could stop this fine vehicle!"

Theresa tried to hide a smile. A mechanical spider like hers in every garage in America seemed a rather silly idea.

"You must think big, Miss Brown," Dr. Flax said, seeming to read her thoughts. "Always think big! Your spider might cut highway traffic in half, which in turn would cut carbon emissions significantly, which in turn would reduce global warming, which in turn would slow down hurricanes. And I think driving a spider would be much more fun than driving a boring old car. Also, I wonder how such a spider would fare on ice . . ."

As soon as Dr. Flax said it, he lost himself in a daydream. Theresa didn't know if she should say something until he finally did.

"Yes," he said slowly. "*On ice.* Tell me, could you give it skis?"

He crawled behind the spider and crouched down to inspect the underbelly.

Skis. Yes, she might be able to give her spider skis. She immediately began to think about how wide they would have to be, where they would fit, and how much weight they would have to bear. Because every time she added something to her spider, she became that much heavier and less agile.

"What do you think? Is there a possibility?" the doctor asked.

Oh. She had forgotten to answer out loud.

"I think skis are a wonderful idea," she said proudly.

Dr. Flax stood up and shook his hair like a happy dog trotting out of a lake.

"Well, then. I'm glad I could help. But now I must leave you because I am soaked. Marie is quite sore with me, as she believes I'll catch a cold. I programmed her to protect the owner of Flax Industries at all costs, but what kind of father would I be if I didn't search for my lost son because of a little rain? But the little rascal continues to elude me, as does the solution to my Big Zero.

"However," he said with a deep and sad sigh, "a robot who does not want to be found will not be found, and the laws of thermodynamics will change for no one—not even me."

Theresa didn't know what to say. She thought it was sweet

that Dr. Flax referred to Thomas as his lost son, just as she thought of her spider as her baby girl.

Dr. Flax perked up and shook his wet overalls one more time.

"I will let you finish installing your grappling hooks, Miss Brown. I'm quite impressed with your work. Zachary is preparing salads. He really makes magic with roasted pecans. A spider builder must not forget to take care of herself. I don't want your father accusing me of starving you. Okay?"

Theresa smiled shyly.

Dr. Flax clapped his hands quietly together.

Then he whispered his thoughts, to her or himself or perhaps to no one at all.

"Imagine a world crawling with gigantic solar-powered spiders equipped with grappling hooks and retractable skis. Wouldn't that be something?"

CHAPTER ELEVEN
SUSTAINABILITY

Moving as slowly as if he had been sentenced by a judge to serve lunches to children until the sun burned out, Zachary carried a platter with three plates of spinach salads topped with apples and roasted pecans, glasses of pineapple juice to drink, and a large wedge of pineapple for dessert.

The plates were as edible as the salads piled upon them, as were the forks and knives. Theresa recognized the utensils and plates from the Flax Inventions for a Better World catalog because they were available for purchase every year. Jon ate his knife right away and was delighted that it tasted like a cinnamon graham cracker. Ashley chastised him for eating his knife first because he had left himself no way to cut his pineapple wedge into more appropriate chewable pieces unless he asked Zachary for another knife, which would probably take him more than an hour to retrieve. Jon didn't care. He wasn't afraid to use his hands during any meal.

They sat in an ornate white gazebo beneath a magnificent skylight. The matching white wrought-iron table where they sat looked familiar to Theresa, as it had been recycled from one of the mall's flower shops. The gazebo was surrounded by banana trees, concentric circles of roses, lemon and lime trees, and finally a ring of red, green, and yellow pepper plants that were just starting to produce. Brilliantly white snowy egrets searched for bugs in a nearby fountain, and there was the ever-present rushing of water through the walls. Theresa had never been in such a beautiful garden, inside or out.

"May I bring you *children* anything else?" Zachary asked with a sigh. He seemed to be annoyed whenever he was required to address them directly. He had replaced his work apron with a kitchen apron, which was also imprinted with the same pineapple and FLAX across the top. They all quietly said, "No, thank you," and he shuffled grumpily away.

"They sure like pineapples here," Jon said before he started shoveling the salad into his mouth like someone was going to snatch it away from him.

"Can you believe this place?" Ashley said to Theresa with genuine awe. "It's like a paradise for environmental scientists." Theresa was relieved when Ashley spoke to her. She thought she might still be mad at her for getting the bigger laboratory.

"I wonder if this will be what the future looks like," Theresa said.

"I hope I have a robot of my own in the future," Jon said.

"I'll make him do all my dirty work while I kick back and make bubbles."

"You'll need to learn how to program robots, then," Ashley replied.

Theresa thought of Thomas Edison, who seemed to need some reprogramming himself.

"Do you think any of these inventions are dangerous?" Theresa asked them. "Like, *really* dangerous? So dangerous they should be destroyed?"

"We're in a laboratory," Ashley said matter-of-factly. "The inventions here aren't ready for the public. They're all in the experimental stage. So of course they could be dangerous."

It was hard for Theresa to imagine anything in this beautiful place being harmful. But Thomas Edison seemed awfully certain *something* here had to be destroyed. She tried to put the thought out of her mind.

Ashley stared at Jon disapprovingly as he ate his salad by the handful.

"What are you two inventing?" Ashley asked, trying to make polite, appropriate conversation.

"I'm making my spider better than ever," Theresa said excitedly. "I want her to shoot grappling hooks and climb. I'm going to add skis to her feet, too."

"Hmm. Not sure how a toy spider makes the world a better place," Ashley said, deflating Theresa's enthusiasm just like that. "What about you, *Buzz*?"

Jon lit up.

"I'm working on a bubble organ! It's gonna be a huge pipe connected to an organ that releases colored bubbles in time with the music you play. And it's going to be massive. The prototype will be three feet long, but then I'm going to ask the doctor if we can build one that's HUGE!"

"Like how big?" Ashley asked.

Jon thought about it. "One hundred feet long!"

Ashley shook her head. "That sounds as useful to environmental science as a spider that can shoot grappling hooks."

"Okay, hotshot," Jon said. "What are you making?"

Ashley cleared her throat proudly.

"Way more Ashley Dean's Edible Algae–brand products. Tortillas, chips, and even cookies made from algae with all different flavors. Maybe even chocolate!"

"So exciting," Jon said sarcastically. "I'm sure everyone will line up for miles to buy chocolate algae cookies."

"Never underestimate the power of a cookie," Dr. Flax said as he appeared from behind a lemon tree. He had dried off and put on a fresh pair of excessively pocketed white overalls. The doctor was very good, it seemed, at appearing unexpectedly.

"How is lunch? To your liking?"

They all nodded enthusiastically.

"Let me introduce a concept for you three to discuss while you eat. Sustainability. Who can define it?"

Theresa's spider was powered by a solar battery. She knew this one.

"Sustainable resources are ones that don't ever run out. Like solar or wind power."

"That's right, Miss Brown! It has another definition I like as well. Jon? Ashley? Hazard a guess?"

Ashley raised her hand confidently, and the doctor pointed to her.

"Sustainable also means to be able to stay the same. To be maintained. To keep something going."

"Very good, Miss Dean! I like your choice of words very much. *To be maintained.*"

Ashley smirked at Theresa like she'd won another point or something. Did this whole summer have to be a competition between them?

"You three finish up your lunches and then, if you would, join me in the flower garden outside your laboratories. I'd like to introduce you to one of my new inventions."

Then he turned and called out toward the kitchen.

"Zachary? Hello, Zach? Is there any salad left?"

"Yes, Uncle," he groaned from the kitchen. "I have a plate waiting for you here. As always."

"Don't forget to eat your forks," the doctor said as he strolled away.

Jon already had.

CHAPTER TWELVE
BEES

The flower garden was a narrow strip of lush and sweet-smelling blooms that stretched from one end of the western wing of the laboratory to the other. It was bursting with yellow jasmine and pink bougainvillea, red roses and orange daisies, and blue wildflowers peeking out through the grasses.

When they arrived, they found Dr. Flax sitting on a large crate in the middle of the stone sidewalk that meandered through the flower beds.

The crate was buzzing.

"Come closer, young colleagues. Nothing to be afraid of."

Theresa didn't know whether to believe him, but the three of them took seats in the grass in front of the doctor and the crate.

"To maintain. To sustain. If our society continues to deplete trees and clean water and other resources without replacing them, and then more and more animals and insects are extinguished due to the lack of those resources, how can we maintain our ecosystem? What if, God forbid, we *don't* transform into a solar-and-wind-powered civilization fast enough? What options will we have?"

"We all go to Mars." Jon shrugged.

Ashley scoffed, but Dr. Flax pointed to him enthusiastically.

"Yes, indeed, Mr. Cooper! If we fail, we will eventually have to find another planet to call home. But that is our most expensive option and, presently, requires technology we do not have."

He patted his hand on the crate, and it buzzed even louder.

"While we wait patiently for our society to make that transition, how can we maintain? Well, for one thing, we will have to replace the most important species on this planet. Any guesses as to what that species might be? I'll eliminate one of them for you—it is not our dear *Homo sapiens*."

Theresa thought she might know. The buzzing crate was a big clue.

"The bee?" she guessed.

"That's right, Miss Brown! Good thinking! The common but quite essential honeybee. Without the honeybee, there is no pollination of our food crops, and without crops we soon perish. However . . ."

With a theatric wave of his hand, Dr. Flax lifted the lid off the crate.

Theresa didn't know whether to step back or step forward to have a look. Before she could decide, hundreds of small

metallic creatures rose out of the crate, buzzing and flying together in a chaotic swarm. The things had silver wings, metallic yellow bodies each with a single black stripe, and very tiny glowing, unnatural red eyes.

They were robotic bees.

Their swarm began to change into an organized and very precise formation. They soon unified to become a buzzing yellow arrow hanging in the air.

And the arrow was pointed directly at Ashley.

"Oh my," the doctor said as he realized their intention.

"Whoa!" Jon yelled in awe. He was loving every second.

"Why are they doing that? Why are they pointing at me?" Ashley asked nervously, stepping backward. As she retreated, the bee arrow advanced toward her. She stepped back three steps, and the arrow of bees buzzed forward three steps.

"Miss Dean," the doctor said cautiously, "perhaps you'd better take cover behind that trellis of bougainvillea. I designed these robotic bees to simulate real bees. They are programmed to seek out contrasts in bright colors and sweet floral scents. They seem to be attracted to the pink polka dots on your blue dress and the very floral perfume you've chosen to wear today."

Ashley screamed. She turned and dived behind the trellis as she covered her head, but the arrow of bees followed her and then swarmed around her body. In only seconds, Ashley was completely covered.

Theresa was horrified.

"Turn them off, Dr. Flax!" Ashley screamed. "TURN THEM OFF!"

The doctor picked up the crate and tried to scoop them out of the air, but to no avail.

"Each bee has its own individual on/off switch on its belly. I'm afraid I can't turn them off collectively. I now very much regret this design flaw."

Ashley screamed again as she crawled around on the ground behind the trellis. The bees covered every inch of her, and it appeared that they might even suffocate her as they covered her nose and mouth.

Then Theresa had an idea.

"Jon, your colored-smoke bubble maker! Go get it!"

Jon jumped up. "Good thinking!"

Jon's laboratory was just one door down from the flower garden, and Theresa's was only four doors farther. Jon ran to get his bubble maker, and Theresa flew to her lab to get the shop vacuum normally used for cleaning up.

"Don't worry, Miss Dean! Don't worry!" the doctor kept shouting as he grabbed the bees, one by one, turning off the switches on their underbellies.

Unfortunately, there were hundreds of them.

"Oh dear," he said. "This will take a while."

Theresa rolled her shop vacuum as fast as she could back to the flower garden, where Ashley was now curled up in a ball screaming into her hands.

Jon returned and stood his bubble maker on its end. Then

he lit the colored incense in each of its inset pods. Soon the large bright bubbles of smoke floated out of the top, colliding with one another, becoming smoky orbs inside smoky orbs. Yellow inside blue. Green inside red. Purple inside orange.

The robotic bees liked these contrasts of colors very much and—slowly but surely—began to turn from Ashley toward the rainbow of smoke bubbles. When the mechanical bees touched them, the bubbles popped, and the bees grew calmer once they were engulfed in the colorful smoke. Theresa searched for a place to plug in her shop vacuum.

"There's an outlet under that turtle," the doctor said urgently, stuffing his pockets with his dysfunctional bees.

Sure enough, when Theresa lifted a box turtle that was sunbathing on a fake rock, she found an outlet. She plugged in the vacuum and began to suck the robotic bees into it. It took a while, but she soon had the bulk of them.

"Well," Dr. Flax said, looking very much relieved. "I count us all fortunate that I hadn't yet given the bees stingers. Miss Dean would have been quite well punctured if I had."

Ashley lay on the ground in a bit of shock with her face still in her hands. She didn't dare open her eyes.

Then she yelled, "AIYEEEEEEE!"

Dr. Flax jumped in surprise at her impressively high-pitched scream.

"All right," he said. "Clearly Miss Dean has been through quite an ordeal. Perhaps that's enough talk about sustainability

and bees. Let's all get back to work on our inventions, shall we?"

The doctor quickly backed away from the scene, and they all returned to their laboratories. Theresa heard Jon burst out with a laugh behind her, but she tried to ignore it for Ashley's sake.

Back in her lab, Theresa finished up the installation of grappling hooks on her spider. She turned up her Disney musical station and was soon lost in her work. But for the rest of the afternoon, she wondered if she should go check on Ashley. She didn't want to embarrass her, though. When she was happy with her spider's new twin web shooters, she gave them a try by firing them at a large cardboard box full of headlamps.

Success! The hooks grabbed hold, and she was able to reel in the box like a spider pulling in its prey. She was quite proud of her work and wanted to show the doctor, but when she looked at the clock, it was already five minutes to five.

She walked out to the front entrance and didn't know what to say when she took her spot next to Ashley and Jon. They stood there quietly, looking out over the pineapple fields, waiting for their parents' cars. Thankfully, breaking the silence, Ashley started giggling for no explicable reason.

"You know," she said, "maybe I should be the one called Buzz."

Jon and Theresa burst into laughter. It wouldn't have been so funny if it hadn't been Ashley who had said it.

CHAPTER THIRTEEN
NO FORKLIFT

Theresa had never seen her father look so relieved.

"Were you worried I wouldn't make it out alive, Dad?"

"The thought had crossed my mind," her father said as he drove them home.

She forced herself to stay quiet.

Theresa wanted so badly to tell her story. How the inside of the laboratory looked like Nature itself had reclaimed the mall with birds and flowers and trees in every possible space. There were waterfalls *inside* the walls, she wanted to say, and the doctor had given her her own laboratory, and it was the *biggest* one, but she didn't want to brag about it because Ashley was jealous, although she thought they could still be friends. Marie Curie was a robot, and the doctor's nephew was like the disgruntled butler or something, and Ashley nearly got suffocated by robotic bees until Theresa and Jon saved her, and the robot kid who tried to sneak into

91

the laboratory? Well, the doctor acts like he's his real son, and he spends every morning looking for him, and the robot kid thinks Marie Curie is his sister! And on top of all that, there's supposedly something really dangerous in the laboratory, but she didn't have time to worry about that because she was having so much fun, and she had mounted swiveling grappling-hook slingshots on her spider and they actually worked!

No, she couldn't tell him any of that.

She was too afraid he'd turn into the panicky dad she knew too well. The dad who would rather she stay home and help him check off the contents of their emergency hurricane kit than do anything slightly, possibly, even remotely dangerous.

"So?" her father asked, because he couldn't stand silence for any time at all. "How was it, then?"

"It was pretty cool," she said without letting herself show too much excitement. "I have my own space to work and all the welding stuff I could ever need. Dr. Flax even gave me a forklift to use."

"A forklift?" Her father gasped, choking on his words and nearly running a red light. He hit the brake and sat there panting. "You can't run a forklift! A forklift? Are you kidding me? Come on, Theresa! That's crazy!"

"Dad," she said evenly, carefully. "I think if I can handle a welding torch on my own, I can drive a simple forklift."

"That's completely different. Your uncle Robert spent *years* teaching you how to weld and honestly, I can't say I'm totally thrilled about that, either. You're twelve years old, no

matter if you think otherwise. Theresa, listen to me—NO FORKLIFT."

"Okay, Dad, okay. I think you're overreacting, but okay. No forklift."

She let her father calm down and breathe for the next three miles.

She smiled and looked out the window. She knew what she was doing. She had a great, thrilling story to tell him, but she couldn't. If she did, his head would explode. Instead, she gave him the forklift. Just a hint of the danger. A little something he could get upset about. Because if she told him the *whole* truth, he for sure would put an end to it all and she'd never be allowed to go back to Flax Industries. Goodbye personal laboratory. Goodbye new friends. Goodbye Dr. Flax and his peculiar robotic children. Goodbye to the chance to stop hurricanes.

But she couldn't hide *everything*. If she did, he wouldn't believe she was being honest.

So she let him go nuts about the forklift. She couldn't imagine ever needing to use it anyway.

"I'm serious," he said as they pulled into their driveway. "I really mean it, Theresa. I'm the grown-up in this family. You can't go back there tomorrow unless you promise me—*no forklift!*"

"Got it, Dad," she said, pretending to sulk. "No forklift."

CHAPTER FOURTEEN

SEE WHERE YOU ARE

The next morning, Theresa installed skis onto her spider.

She had spent the whole night planning. Her original idea was to attach eight little skis to her spider's eight double-jointed legs, which would be lowered by pulling eight individual levers. But like a lot of designs that are drawn furiously in the excitement of initial inspiration, Theresa quickly realized that this would not go well in implementation. So she spent the first thirty minutes of her morning in her laboratory pacing around her spider in frustration.

Then she realized it would be much easier to simply have two skis unfold and drop down from her spider's underbelly with the pull of one single lever. It was a much simpler design and more practical to build—two promising signs.

She found all the supplies she would need on the first floor. She uncovered two brand-new child-size water skis that would fit perfectly. She also found two new propellers that she could add to the skis to move the spider forward when on water.

The next step was to create the lever that would drop the skis down when she pulled it. Hours disappeared as she designed and cut and welded. She made three levers that didn't work at all until her fourth model did the trick. She was on her back beneath her spider singing along with "A Whole New World," making the final adjustments, when she saw a pair of shoes to her left.

Jon had strolled into her lab. He bent down to see what she was doing.

"Water skis?"

"Or snow skis," Theresa said. "Not sure when or where I'll get to try them out."

"Oh, I know where," Jon said slyly.

She scrambled out from beneath her spider.

"Where? You mean leave Flax Industries?"

"No, of course not," Jon said. "Haven't you gone exploring yet?"

Theresa hadn't even considered leaving her lab without a chaperone. Dr. Flax had said mornings were for working on their inventions.

Jon shook his head in disbelief.

"You're inside the most famous and mysterious laboratory in the world, Theresa Brown. You've got to see where you are! C'mon. Let's take your skiing spider for a test drive. I know just the place."

CHAPTER FIFTEEN
BEWARE OF THE PURIGATOR

C an I drive?" Jon asked, already jumping behind the steering wheel.

Except for the science fair judges, Theresa had never let anyone drive her spider before. No one had ever asked. Why hadn't Darby, Tameka, or Kayla ever wanted to? She suddenly felt a wave of sadness but excitement, too, like she'd moved to a new state where she missed her old friends but found herself making new ones. She felt like—maybe—she had found her people.

"Sure," she said. "See how it has a forward pedal and a reverse? You turn the wheel to go left or right and, well, that's it really. Let's get Ashley before we go."

Jon gave her a look that meant Ashley would ruin all the fun.

"There's only room on this spider for two," Jon said.

"I'll run alongside it," Theresa said. There was no way she was going to be the mean girl and leave Ashley out. No—she refused to be that.

"Fine," Jon groaned, and as if he had done it a hundred times before, he pressed on the forward pedal and turned the wheel. With a *clickety-clickety-click-click-clickety-clickety-click-click*, he lunged forward.

"Whoa! This spider can go!"

"Twelve miles an hour at top speed," she said proudly.

Jon wouldn't crash into anything, would he? Was this a horrible idea? Luckily, he was driving in a relatively straight line down the walkway. Five painted buntings flew out of his way, and a gray heron launched off the upper-level handrail when Jon yelled, "*Wahoo!*"

Theresa had to admit, she liked that he liked it.

Ashley's lab was three doors to the right. Jon pretended he didn't know that. Theresa could tell he fully intended to drive right by. But as they neared her door, they heard the sound of music.

Ashley was playing "The Sorcerer's Apprentice" from the musical *Fantasia*. It was one of Theresa's favorite Disney musicals.

Theresa couldn't help herself. She jumped out of the passenger seat and ran into Ashley's lab.

Ashley was in her own world with "The Sorcerer's Apprentice" as her soundtrack. She was waving her hands like

a conductor and using an eyedropper to give tiny lunches to her rainbow-colored algae.

"I love this song!" Theresa yelled and Ashley jumped.

"You scared me!"

Theresa came closer to look in her aquariums. She had never found algae worth looking at before, but Ashley's glimmered in the water like floating aliens of all colors—rusty reds and fluorescent greens and the very deepest of blues. In the bottom of one of the aquariums was a plastic Mickey Mouse wearing the sorcerer's cap.

"I listen to Disney when I'm working, too," Theresa said.

Ashley smiled and said quietly, "This symphony makes me feel like I'm the apprentice and these algae are my magic brooms." But then, remembering that Theresa was supposed to be her competition, she hid her smile and returned to dropping food into the aquariums.

But Theresa would not let her escape so easily.

"We're going exploring, Ashley. Want to come?"

Ashley spun on her heel with a stare that Theresa had already grown to expect from her—critical and disapproving.

"You're supposed to be working on your invention. Don't you want to win?"

"Win what?"

"*Win what?*" Ashley mimicked in disbelief. "To win the chance to have your invention be in next year's Flax Inventions for a Better World catalog!"

Theresa shrugged. "I didn't think we were here to win or lose."

Ashley shook her head and said, "Those are the words of a loser."

Theresa had been called *strange* and *weird* and *abnormally shy* and even *a hermit*, but never once had she been called *a loser*.

How many times, she wondered, should you try to be friends with someone who is simply downright dead set on being mean? Even if it's the right thing to do, how many times should you ignore someone determined to be your enemy?

You can't force someone to be your friend, right?

"Okay, fine then," Theresa said curtly. "See you later."

Theresa turned and hopped back into the passenger seat of the spider. Jon gave Theresa a look that said, *I told you so*, and then pressed the forward pedal all the way down.

They passed door after door, some with intriguing names above them, some with none at all. Theresa was worried Zachary would step out from behind a tree at any second to reprimand them. Although maybe he didn't care what they did and where they went. It was Miss Curie who seemed to worry they might be a threat to productivity or the lab or, most of all, to Dr. Flax himself.

But then they heard a voice behind them.

"Hey, wait! Stop!"

Theresa looked over her shoulder to see Ashley standing outside her lab.

Maybe she was worried about them.

Maybe she just wanted to scold them again.

Maybe she had changed her mind and wanted to come along but didn't know how to ask.

Jon stepped off the forward pedal, looking at Theresa, expecting her to give Ashley one more chance.

"Well?" Jon asked her.

"Keep going," Theresa said sharply, turning back around so she couldn't see Ashley.

Jon pressed the forward pedal. Theresa couldn't be sure, but she thought Ashley was still standing there, watching them spider-walk away.

After they passed the front entrance and the large fountain basin where the one-eyed duck was still swimming in a circle, the interior landscape began to change. The western wing— where their laboratories were—was like a botanical garden full of tweeting birds and flowers of all colors. But when they entered the eastern wing, Theresa felt like she was back on Folly Beach. This wing was landscaped more like a South Carolina marsh. There was spartina grass and palmetto trees and even dark, thick pluff mud between the two walkways. Theresa saw clumps of oysters peeking out of the mud and thought she saw a rat snake slither into the shadows. It was very quiet on this end except for the ever-present rushing of water in the walls.

Jon took his foot off the pedal, and the spider came to a halt.

"It's so peaceful here," Theresa said quietly. "I like it."

A mosquito landed on her arm. She would normally have smacked it, but it seemed wrong to hurt even a mosquito in this perfectly designed laboratory.

But mosquitoes? Really? Couldn't Dr. Flax have built his paradise without those annoying things? The mosquito filled up with blood, flew away, and Theresa watched the bite on her arm rise to a red bump.

A grove of southern live oak trees grew between the walkways where, Theresa remembered, there had once been a kiosk that sold mechanical dogs. The dogs were cute toys that could walk and bark and lift their front paws. Theresa had convinced her father to buy her one at age four—soon after her mother had been lost to the flood. She had loved that dog so much that she took it apart to see how it worked. She wanted to make it bigger. With her uncle Robert's help, she did, and she had built a new robotic dog twice as big that could walk twice as fast. She'd installed the voice box from the original dog to give it the same bark.

That dog had been her first mechanical creation. It was also the first robot that had helped her forget about the black hole that lived inside her. Theresa had named the dog Lucky after a Dalmatian from her favorite book.

And even though that memory and Lucky had been very real, these live oaks seemed to be so firmly rooted, it was easy to believe they had always been there, before Flax Industries or even the Paper Mill Mall. They were proof that if only

given the chance, Nature could return to any place stronger than it had been before.

The live oak branches rose all the way to the skylights, two stories up. As they came closer, Theresa thought she saw the shimmer of water beyond them.

"Let's check it out," she whispered.

Jon drove the spider slowly through the grove and the marsh beyond. The spider's pointed legs made it quite easy to move through the mud. Soon they saw an expansive lake stretched out before them. It was emerald green, and sunlight danced off the surface.

"I knew there had to be a lake in here," Jon whispered as loud as he dared.

"You did not," Theresa said.

"I did too! What with the water in the walls? I knew there had to be a source somewhere."

"The source could be outside."

"Well, it's not; it's right here. So let's go waterskiing!"

Jon was about to drive the spider right through the marsh grass and into the lake until Theresa whispered, "Wait! What about the Purigator?"

"What's a Purigator?" Jon asked.

Theresa pointed to a sign twenty feet away.

Jon squinted and read the words out loud.

"BEWARE OF THE PURIGATOR. Huh. Sounds fake. Let's go!"

CHAPTER SIXTEEN
THE PURIGATOR

Theresa's heart was pumping. They probably should have taken the time to figure out what a Purigator might be, but she couldn't wait to see if her spider could ski.

"I want to be the first to drive her into the lake!" she said, so she and Jon switched seats.

They walked slowly into the water, going deeper and deeper until the water was nearly to the top of her spider's legs.

She turned to Jon and quietly asked, "Ready?"

He was so ready, he was about to pop out of his orange shirt.

She pressed the forward pedal.

Twelve miles an hour on water seemed a lot faster than on land. The weight of the propellers on the backs of the skis caused the spider to lean back, but to compensate, Theresa and Jon leaned forward. The propellers caught the water and launched them ahead and suddenly . . . they were skiing.

Her design had worked! They were zooming right across the lake. They both screamed in delight.

"This baby can really go!" Jon yelled.

Then, as they reached the far end of the lake, they saw it.

"Look!" Theresa said, hitting Jon on the shoulder.

What used to be Headley's, the big department store that was once two floors of the latest fashions, appliances, and patio furniture, was now shielded by a monolithic steel door with large, recycled letters above it that read THE BIG ZERO.

"That's it!" Theresa shouted above the roar of the propellers. "That's where Dr. Flax works on his magnum opus—his invention that will stop hurricanes!"

They leaned back to take in the view of the gigantic steel gate.

And that's exactly when the spider flipped backward, sending them both upside down, head over heels into the water.

Even as Theresa tumbled down to the bottom of the lake, she wondered how she could improve the obvious design flaw. The propellers had made the spider too heavy on her backside. If she were to widen the skis and place lead bumpers on the front ends, then the weight of the spider would be more evenly distributed. Toppling over would be less likely.

But first she had to keep herself from drowning. Growing up in a town surrounded on all sides by water had given her decent swimming skills, allowing her to quickly right herself and shoot to the surface just in time to see Jon's head pop up.

"That was cool!" he screamed. "I think I touched the bottom!"

"I told you two you were gonna die!"

Ashley had followed them after all and was yelling at them from the west end of the lake.

"Oh, jeez, calm down! We're fine," Jon shouted.

But then Ashley screamed, "LOOK OUT!" with her hands cupped around her mouth.

Theresa turned to look.

In the middle of the lake, just above the surface of the water, two glowing red eyes had seen them. Then the water began to ripple as the eyes started moving toward them. As the thing came closer, Theresa could see it had the head of an alligator and moved like one—slowly and with the determination of an animal that was hungry.

"Let's get out of here," Theresa said urgently. "Let's get out NOW!"

Jon agreed and started swimming backward. Theresa launched herself toward shore, trying not to panic.

The silver alligator chose to follow her.

It was the Purigator, as the sign had warned them. When its back broke the surface, Theresa could see that its scales were actually reflective solar panels. Its tail swished back and forth like a rudder. Bubbles were released out of its behind as it "ate" whatever it found, grinding the pollutant into mush, filtering the liquid, and leaving only pure water in its wake, eliminating what did not belong.

Theresa and Jon did not belong.

"Get out of there!" Ashley screamed.

Theresa looked over her shoulder to see if the Purigator was gaining on her. It definitely was. But in that split second, she saw him. He stood in front of his lab, below his name spelled out in large, uniform black steel letters—ZACHARY. With his hands behind his back, he watched them struggle. He didn't offer help; he didn't show concern.

He didn't even bother to advise Theresa to swim faster.

She could feel the Purigator getting closer, the waves of its movement getting bigger. Then she heard its jaws unhinge—*creeeaaak*.

This would be a very unpleasant way to die.

But suddenly—*splash!*

Dr. Flax had thrown off his Sensory Amplifier and cannonballed himself into the water. He soon had his arms around the Purigator's neck, tumbling it upside down and then sliding himself over its belly until they were both underwater. He had given Theresa just enough time to swim to the opposite side.

Jon and Theresa ran along the edge of the lake, looking for him, yelling, "Dr. Flax! Dr. Flax!"

Zachary continued watching from his post, not bothered in the slightest.

Then Dr. Flax broke the surface of the water, riding the Purigator's back like he was a rodeo cowboy on a bucking bronco.

"I'm afraid he doesn't care for me," the doctor said as he gripped the metal gator with his knees. "He doesn't like intruders of any kind, really. That's how I designed him. And although I was born and raised in Charleston, I regret to say I'm not an accomplished swimmer."

The Purigator wouldn't let the doctor overturn it again. When he moved left, it moved left, and when the doctor moved right, the Purigator compensated. The jaws began to unhinge again, and now Theresa could see that Dr. Flax had given his creation not one but five rows of sharp teeth to slash through any garbage it found.

Ashley jumped in the water.

"What are you doing?" Theresa yelled at her.

Ashley had a large baggie in her hand. She opened it up and threw it high in the air so that it came down with a splat on the Purigator's back, the contents spilling all around it.

The baggie contained a large specimen of her algae that quickly began to spread in circles on the surface of the water around the mechanical beast.

The Purigator immediately changed its focus and got to work. It started chomping at the algae, moving efficiently in increasing concentric circles, eating all the slime polluting the lake, just as it had been programmed to.

Dr. Flax dog-paddled away and was soon wading out of the water.

"Well done, Miss Dean! Very quick thinking! It will take

my dear Purigator a good ten minutes to eat all your algae. How smart to keep some with you!"

"But really weird," Jon said. "Do you always keep algae in your pocket?"

"Always," Ashley said without even looking at him. "And you should thank me for it."

Jon wrung out his shirt and only chuckled to himself.

"Thank you, Ashley," Theresa said seriously. "That was really good thinking."

"Hmm" was her only reply.

Jon gave Dr. Flax a hand to help him out of the lake. The doctor sat on a large stone in the mud to catch his breath. When Theresa looked to the opposite side, Zachary had disappeared.

Marie Curie, however, spun on her wheel down the path toward them, concerned only for the doctor's safety.

"Are you all right, sir? Did the children put you in danger? Do you have any injuries that need attending?"

She was carrying a large towel, which she quickly wrapped around the doctor. She did not have any towels for the children, nor did she seem to care.

"I'm fine, Marie. I'm fine. Miss Dean demonstrated quick thinking and kept the Purigator from eating me. Don't mind me, now. Our colleagues and I should have our daily discussion."

"But what about Thomas Edison?" Marie whispered.

Dr. Flax let out a big sigh.

"Yes. I have good news to report, everybody. Marie and I have found Tommy. He was in the pineapple fields this morning, but he once again ran off and escaped us. My poor sweet boy—I could not catch him. Go and look for him, Marie. Try to convince your brother to come home. I will follow you shortly. But these young inventors deserve my attention, too."

As Miss Curie rolled reluctantly off to look for her brother, Dr. Flax led them several feet away to a short stone wall that kept the pluff mud and grass from spilling out onto the walkway.

"Have a seat, my friends, and let's talk for a few minutes. Shall we?"

It would have been nice if they could get some dry clothes or at least some towels before they began their discussion, but the doctor seemed too preoccupied to think of it.

CHAPTER SEVENTEEN

PRACTICALITY

What does *practicality* mean? Anyone?"

Ashley's hand went up immediately. Dr. Flax nodded for her to answer.

"How usable something is in real life. Like, is it convenient or inconvenient?"

"Yes, indeed," he said as Ashley smiled pompously. It was difficult to find her annoying at this moment, however, considering she had just saved them from being eaten.

"When an idea for an invention comes to me," the doctor said, "I first consider only *possibility*. Could my idea become a real thing? One day I imagined an alligator that purified the water as it swam. Then I asked myself, how could I build it? Well, I modeled my design after a real alligator. Then I gave it a waterproof motor, solar panel scales for energy, a replaceable belly bag to contain the garbage it would eat, and a water purifier in its rump. Possibility was followed by implementation, and lo and behold, the Purigator was born!"

Then Dr. Flax became silent and shut his eyes and quietly clapped his hands together, just as he had in Theresa's laboratory. He took a very long time with his thoughts, and after a while, it was clear Jon was trying to keep himself from laughing. Finally, the doctor opened his eyes and continued.

"But now I must ask myself, is the Purigator practical? Perhaps I should have posed this question long before I built him, because now that he exists, I'm quite fond of him. I naturally want to share him with the world. But should I? Should I include the Purigator in next year's Flax Inventions for a Better World catalog?"

Ashley raised her hand, but this was a rhetorical question. Theresa and Jon waited while the doctor lost himself in thought again, and Ashley slowly, awkwardly dropped her hand back down to her lap.

"Perhaps none of my inventions are practical." Dr. Flax sighed. "My bees swarmed Miss Dean because she was wearing a polka-dot dress. My Purigator tried to eat us because he saw us as pollutants. My sweet little Tommy, who was programmed to help me save the planet from climate change, thinks my greatest invention is instead our world's greatest danger. Clearly, my fantasy to seclude myself in a beautiful laboratory to create inventions without being disturbed

by the world has become just that—a fantasy completely removed from the planet I'm trying to save."

He became very quiet and looked at the children expectantly. Were they supposed to speak this time? Ashley didn't dare try again. But Theresa, wanting to break the awkward silence before it became truly unbearable or Jon started laughing, said, "Um . . . well?"

Then Dr. Flax seemed to suddenly find himself. He stood up and began to abruptly and unsuccessfully wipe the mud from his overalls.

"Excuse me, young scientists. It serves no purpose—indeed, it is not *practical*—to sit and dwell on one's own shortcomings. I must continue my search for Tommy and try to fix what I have broken. And you have your own inventions to work on, don't you?"

The doctor lapsed into contemplative silence again but then regarded each of them with an adoring smile.

"You know, I've quickly grown to admire you three. You're all quite clever. Perhaps you'll find success in this laboratory where I have not."

And with that, Dr. Flax began to limp away. He must have hurt his ankle when he jumped onto the Purigator.

"Maybe I'll take a long nap," he said to no one in particular as he moved slowly down the walkway toward the western wing, leaving a trail of mud behind him.

Theresa felt quite bad for him and thought she should say

or do *something*. Before he walked too far, she mustered up the courage.

"What about your magnum opus? What about your Big Zero? What about stopping hurricanes?"

Dr. Flax paused and turned to consider the three enormous and daunting words at the eastern end of the laboratory— THE BIG ZERO.

"Perhaps my greatest invention isn't so great after all. It may be impractical or—like so many of my machines here— dangerously unsafe. Yes, Miss Brown, I will have to reconsider that and many other things."

Then he returned to limping down the walkway and was soon gone.

Theresa wanted to do something for him. She couldn't see why he should be so down on himself. This laboratory was unlike anything she had ever imagined—a huge, self-sustaining botanical paradise powered by the sun and cooled by water in the walls with rooms devoted to botany and robotics and engineering and even bubble science (if that was a thing). Flax Industries was the most beautiful place Theresa had ever been.

She wanted to tell him so. She wanted to tell Dr. Flax that he had created plenty of practical inventions! Like his Bionic Baby Bottom Buffer and his External Lie Detector and even his Sensory Amplifier . . . which she now realized was lying in the mud right where Dr. Flax had dropped it.

CHAPTER EIGHTEEN
THE SENSORY AMPLIFIER

Theresa couldn't resist.

She picked up the Sensory Amplifier. It really did look like nothing more than a simple and flimsy fencing mask for a head much larger than hers.

"Let me try it!" Jon said, moving to pull it from her hands.

"You two really shouldn't play with things you don't understand," Ashley said condescendingly. "Five minutes ago, you both were nearly eaten by the Purigator. Don't even think that I'll try to save you again."

But Theresa jerked the Sensory Amplifier away from Jon and lifted it above her head. It was just too tempting to see how it worked.

She slid it on.

Three seconds later, the mask suctioned itself to her face. She thought she was suffocating. For a few anxious moments, she wanted to pull it off, but she made herself breathe and relax. After the mask had finished tightening around the contours of her head, she realized she was in no danger.

Jon said again, "Let me try it, Theresa!"

His words boomed in her head like cannons firing.

Again, he seemed to shout through a bullhorn, "LET ME TRY!"

She instinctively put her hands to her ears. But the mask seemed to be tuning itself to her particular eardrums. The next time he spoke, his words were loud and crisp but bearable.

The grid of the mask faded away from her sight. As her eyes adjusted, the scene around her remained the same and yet completely different. The colors of the flowers and trees and rocks were more vivid than before—not as if they had changed, really, but more like she had never noticed how strong and bright they had always been. When she looked across the surface of the lake, it seemed bluer, brighter, and sparkling with magical light. She could see every single ripple of water, every crack in every stone on the lake's bottom, and every blade of grass surrounding it.

She inhaled a big breath through her nose. She smelled the pungent but rich stink of the pluff mud. She had grown up in the South Carolina marsh and had always known that smell, but now it seemed thicker and so much sweeter. She could smell Ashley's floral perfume, too. It was powerful—*too powerful*—and not exactly pleasant.

The golden sensory gloves would be the final touch to this amazing experience, but Jon had found them first. He had

put them on and was busy feeling the bark of a palmetto tree, completely mesmerized.

When Theresa turned to look at Ashley, the sight of her was almost too much, as if a cloudy screen had been removed from Ashley's whole being, leaving her true self completely exposed. Theresa could see every pore of her skin, every wrinkle of her frown, every crevasse of her furrowed brow. She could almost physically *feel* Ashley's disapproval and—something else there. Jealousy maybe. Theresa could feel Ashley's humming, fretting, stomach-twisting anxiety. She usually came off so confident, but with the Sensory Amplifier on, Theresa sensed her continually twitching nose and shuffling feet. Was she always this nervous?

The mask somehow allowed her to feel Ashley's feelings—like she worried that she didn't belong here and that she wasn't smart enough and that she wasn't . . . *liked*.

Those were all emotions quite familiar to Theresa. She woke up with them every day, and sometimes they kept her up at night. She had an overwhelming desire to give Ashley a hug.

But then she heard something—like a whisper echoing through a canyon.

"Please leave him alone. I'm begging you—*please*! He doesn't *want* to be found. And besides, the daily hunts for Tommy are distracting the doctor. Isn't that what you want? If you let Tommy keep hiding, then the doctor will keep searching, and then you'll be free to do whatever you want!"

It was Marie Curie's voice, somewhere far away but scared . . . and desperate.

Then the Sensory Amplifier picked up another voice—one laced with cruelty, uncompromising harshness, and anger.

"Don't patronize me, *young lady*. Thomas doesn't want to be found because he wants to sneak in here and destroy the real important work of this laboratory. Your little brother is a menace! If I get my hands on him, I'll dismantle him and use him for spare parts. He's outdated and flawed and of no use to anyone. I've only let him exist out of mercy to you and your misplaced sentimentality."

It was the voice of Zachary Flax—but the Sensory Amplifier made his voice darker, harsher, *meaner*.

"I know you have, sir, and I thank you for your kindness." Marie's voice echoed softly and ever so meekly.

"You just keep your promise or I'll go find your brother myself and put an end to this silly distraction. The doctor may have forgotten what's most important to Flax Industries, *but I haven't*. You know, if this nonsense continues, the doctor may have to go, too."

"No! Don't say that! I've already lost my brother. I can't lose my father, too!"

Theresa felt a heavy silence. Then . . . was Miss Curie crying? Could robots cry? And worse, Theresa could almost physically feel Zachary's energy. His cruelty was heavy and suffocating like a barbed blanket. He seemed to be enjoying Miss Curie's pain.

Then Zachary laughed—*loudly*. Theresa spun around, half expecting to find him standing directly behind her. But there was only the rippling of the water and Jon. Jon's eyes were so crystallized by the Sensory Amplifier that she could see every shade of blue, green, brown, and gold in his irises.

"C'mon, Theresa! Let me try it now! It's my turn," Jon said, his voice booming in her ears.

Theresa took off the helmet gladly. It was a relief as sounds softened and the grass and water dimmed to normal, acceptable shades. She took a deep breath. She felt like she had walked out of a loud 3D IMAX movie theater back into the calm, normal shape of real life.

Jon slid on the mask.

Then he screamed and quickly ripped it off.

"What happened?" Ashley asked.

Jon started panting.

"That was the worst thing ever!"

"What?" Theresa gasped.

"I put it on, and I heard Zachary say, *I see you and everything you're doing.* That totally creeped me out!"

"Wait until I tell you two what I heard!" Theresa said.

CHAPTER NINETEEN
BONNIE

The doctor may have to go, too, Zachary had said. But what did he mean by that? He'd kick his uncle out of his own lab?

But Miss Curie seemed genuinely afraid of him, like he really would eliminate Thomas and even Dr. Flax if he thought it was necessary. Zachary seemed like nothing more than a grumpy butler who'd rather be anywhere else, but what if he was protecting the very invention that would change the world forever while the doctor was distracted looking for his lost son?

What if it was Zachary who would return a balance to the climate and ensure the end of hurricanes?

"Dad?" Theresa asked when they were halfway home.

"Yeah, baby girl?"

"If I ran away, how long would you look for me?"

Her father was horrified.

"You're not watching the road, Dad."

"Theresa! How could you even ask that? I would look for you every day and every night. I would never stop until I found you."

She was quiet for a minute.

"I mean, what if it was, like, becoming obvious that I didn't want to be found? How long would you look? For days, months . . . years? Even if you knew I was trying as hard as I could to run away?"

"Theresa," he said. "You're scaring me. Why are you asking me this?"

Theresa wasn't sure herself.

"Yes," her father said. "I would give up everything. My job wouldn't matter. Eating and sleeping wouldn't matter. I would do everything to find you, and I'd do everything I could to understand why you didn't want to come home to me, and then I'd make sure I never lost you again."

He was breathing fast. He was gripping the steering wheel. Still, she couldn't help asking more.

"But what if, Dad, for some reason, you were given only two real choices—to save the planet or to find me? Think about it for a second. You might lose me forever, but you could potentially save hundreds—maybe thousands!—from losing their homes or drowning or being swept away."

He pulled the car over into a gas station and parked. When her father looked at her, he was serious.

"Nothing matters more to me than you, Theresa. Don't

you know that? Nothing else, *no one else.* I lost your mother. I blame myself for that and I probably always will. I *refuse* to ever lose you, no matter what. Okay? Now, Theresa, tell me the truth—is everything all right?"

She was trying to figure out if it was possible to love a robot as much as a child. Could you think of a robot as a child? She loved her spider. But did she love her like Dr. Flax loved Thomas Edison?

What if her spider could talk?

What if she could think?

What if one day her spider tried to run away from Theresa for reasons of her own?

She realized she had forgotten to answer her father. His eyes were welling up with tears.

"Dad. Stop. I'm sorry."

"You know that I love you, Theresa. Right? You know that?"

"Yes, Daddy. I know that. I love you, too."

He wiped his eyes and took a deep breath.

"Tell me this and be honest. Is there something about the laboratory I should know?"

Oh, man. Panicking. She should have never started with these questions. Now she had to give him something. Like the forklift. If she said nothing was the matter, he wouldn't believe her. If she told him the whole truth, his mind would be blown, and he'd never let her return to Flax Industries.

"It's just that . . . Dr. Flax loves that robot boy very much.

And he seems like he cares more about finding him and fixing him than working on his invention that will stop hurricanes. That's all."

"Well," her father said, pulling the car out of the gas station and back into traffic. "Nothing wrong with that. I still can't believe that boy is a robot. He must seem very real to the doctor. Just like your spider seems so real to you and me."

"What?" Theresa couldn't believe what she was hearing. "My spider seems real . . . *to you?*"

Her father started laughing instead of freaking out, which was a relief.

"Of course she does! You love her so much. You're always tinkering with her and talking to her. She's your baby, just like you're mine. I half expect her to talk back to you someday. She's quite something, you know. You should be proud of her. You should be proud of yourself for building her."

Theresa started giggling. "*She?* You think my spider's a girl?"

"Well," her father said, "what do you think?"

Theresa already knew. "Yeah. She's a girl."

"She needs a name, though. How about Miss Spider?"

"Dad! That's a horrible name!"

"What? Seriously? Miss Spider was one of the best characters in *James and the Giant Peach*! I thought you'd appreciate the literary reference."

No, the truth was, Theresa already had a name in mind. Maybe it had been floating in her thoughts for some time.

"I like *Bonnie*. After Mom. I don't know if Mom would have wanted a robot spider named after her, but I want to call her Bonnie."

Then her dad's tears really did come.

"She would have absolutely loved that, baby girl."

Theresa wished she had driven Bonnie home that night. She missed her. She was excited for tomorrow morning at the lab. She thought she might install a spring (or maybe multiple springs) that would allow Bonnie to jump. At least a few feet to clear small objects. Although the more she added, the heavier she would grow and so would become that much more difficult to launch. Especially if she was carrying a driver and a passenger.

Theresa was up very late researching possible jumping mechanisms on her computer when there was a familiar sound at her window.

Tap, tap, tap.

This time, she threw open the window.

"Thomas Edison! Where have you been? Do you know Dr. Flax has been looking for you every day?"

Thomas was still dressed in his puffy winter coat, gloves, and hat. He stood on the top rung of his ladder looking as serious as ever.

"I know," he said urgently. "But even though I can't explain

right now, you have to understand that if the doctor knew what I needed to destroy—"

"He thinks of you like a son! Do you know how worried he is about you?"

Thomas paused for a second.

"I know," he said. "And I love him very much."

"Then why do you keep running away? Talk to him!"

"Because that would put Marie in danger," Thomas whispered. "I think you'll understand after you see what I must destroy. Please, all I ask is that tomorrow you let me in."

Then the ladder started vibrating and Thomas nearly fell off.

They both looked down.

Theresa's father was standing at the bottom, giving the ladder a good shake.

"I see you, Thomas Edison!" her father said. "Any boy who wants to talk to my daughter needs to ring the front doorbell. Robot or not!"

Thomas looked back at Theresa with desperation in his glowing blue eyes.

"Tomorrow," he said. "Promise me you'll let me in. If you do, I promise to explain everything to you *and* my father *and* my sister."

Her father shook the ladder again.

"Young man! I'm talking to you!"

Then, to Theresa's surprise, Thomas bent his knees down, and Theresa could hear the slow whine of something

pressurizing. Thomas bent down farther and pressed two release valves on his knees.

Then he launched . . . up onto the roof.

"Hey!" her father yelled, but Thomas was already running. He scurried to the far side of the roof, jumped into their largest live oak tree, then tumbled down through the branches until he finally hit the ground right on his head.

Theresa hurried downstairs to their porch to see if he was okay. But he had already picked himself up and had run halfway down the street.

CHAPTER TWENTY
PINEAPPLES

As they drove to Flax Industries the next morning, Theresa thought about Thomas's pressurized boots. They certainly worked well for a three-foot-tall boy with two feet. Could she build something similar for a spider with eight feet that ended in points?

She decided that would be her project for the morning. She couldn't wait to get started.

But when they arrived and Theresa saw Miss Curie at the front door with her arms crossed, she sensed that today might not go as she had planned.

"You think she's all right?" her father asked as they pulled in.

"Yeah," Theresa assured him. "She's normally like that. All business."

But something was different.

Miss Curie waited until Theresa's father had driven

completely out of sight before she said, "We will wait here for the others."

"Actually, I'm ready to get started. I wanted to find something to use to make my spider jump. I was thinking about maybe eight pressurized boots, one for each foot—"

"You won't be working in your laboratory today," Miss Curie said curtly, and it was clear that Theresa shouldn't protest.

They stood waiting for Ashley and Jon without a single word said between them. Ashley arrived first, and when she stepped out of her parents' car, she immediately understood she should also be quiet. Jon arrived late, of course, and Miss Curie stared daggers at his raucous family's van until it, too, was out of sight.

"What's going on?" Jon whispered to Theresa, but she was too scared to guess.

Miss Curie said, "Follow me, children," and they did.

She led them to a room on the first floor of the eastern wing named LEATHER. Theresa was surprised there would be such a laboratory at Flax Industries. She couldn't imagine Dr. Flax would ever deliberately harm a cow or an alligator or any other animal whose skin could be fashioned into suitcases or shoes. But when Miss Curie pressed the secret code into the rainbow-colored thirteen-wedge animal-combo lock, the steel gate opened to reveal no animals of any kind.

Theresa knew this place. It had once been a Mexican restaurant called Cha Cha's where Theresa and her father would often have a later dinner on days he worked. They would

127

drink virgin piña coladas and eat so many complimentary chips, they couldn't finish their enchilada plates. But then they would order sopaipillas anyway. It had been one of her mother's favorite places, too. That's what her father said every time they went.

All that remained of the restaurant were the brightly painted tables and chairs bolted to the floor and the colorful mosaic of a bull munching grass in a sunny field.

But now, all the furniture—the tables, the chairs, the bar—was covered with piles and piles of pineapples.

"Quite a lot of fruit, isn't it?" Miss Curie said with a chuckle that made them all immediately suspicious. "Let me show you what's in the other room."

Miss Curie opened the door to the large banquet hall that had once been used for private parties. A machine as long as the room stretched out before them. At one end of the machine was a large, gaping mouth of steel teeth. At the other was a chute with a whole assortment of sprayers and heating elements. The center was a long brass tube with a digital display and a window allowing you to see inside. A conveyor belt ran through the whole thing, from teeth to chute.

Next to the toothy end was a basket of pineapple tops.

Miss Curie turned to face Theresa, Ashley, and Jon.

"Allow me to introduce you to one of Dr. Flax's most brilliant inventions—the Flax Fiberweaverator."

"The what?" Jon asked.

"I know," Miss Curie said, holding her clipboard to her chest, "it's not the best name, but our pineapple-leather fashions are some of our most profitable products, second only to the Bionic Baby Bottom Buffer. You've seen our pineapples growing outside. At Flax Industries, we use every single bit of the plant. Humans like yourselves eat the fruit and the remaining ruffage we put in this machine."

She flipped a switch on the Flax Fiberweaverator, and its digital display lit up, the conveyor belt began to roll, and its steel teeth started gnashing. Then Miss Curie picked up a handful of pineapple tops and threw them in. The Fiberweaverator shredded them instantly, and Miss Curie invited them to come take a closer look through the window.

"The Fiberweaverator chews the leaves into a fine pulp. Then the pulp is soaked, cured, mashed, heated, soaked again, sprayed with salts and other protective minerals, and finally dyed with natural pigments. All in seven minutes and forty-two seconds."

They patiently waited for seven minutes and forty-two seconds.

Then the Fiberweaverator dinged like a toaster, and out of the chute rolled a strip of beautiful indigo-colored pineapple leather.

"You see? One cruelty-free sturdy piece of leather to wear as a belt. Suitable for both boys and girls. Who would like this one?"

Ashley was wearing a dress again (no polka-dots this time)

and Theresa's shorts didn't have belt loops, so Jon took it and replaced the belt he was wearing.

"Cool," he said excitedly. "It says 'Flax' on it."

Miss Curie brought their attention to the far wall where aprons and shoes and briefcases and hats all hung from hooks. They were all imprinted with the brand FLAX.

"You are welcome to take any of these home as souvenirs to show family and friends how productive you were this summer. The leather you make will be sent to our talented tailors right here in Charleston, just a few blocks away. If you work hard and make enough leather, maybe we can visit their shop on the last day of your internship."

Ashley raised her hand politely.

"Yes, Miss Dean?"

"Excuse me, but what do you mean by leather *we* make?"

Miss Curie smiled wickedly and nodded toward a table and three chairs in the adjacent room. On the table lay three butcher knives and three pineapple cutters.

Miss Curie made a note on her clipboard with her pen and calmly waved her hand, suggesting they take a seat.

"Our new manager has determined that you three would better serve Flax Industries by working in this room. You will cut the tops off pineapples and carve out the fruit for human consumption. You will put the tops in the Fiberweaverator to make Flax leather. *You will do this for the remainder of the summer.*"

Then Miss Curie rolled slowly toward them and bent

forward so that her glowing green eyes were level with theirs. Ashley tried to shrink into her shoes, and even Jon seemed to lose his voice. She came nose to nose with Theresa, who so badly wanted to curl into a ball. But she didn't break eye contact.

"When you are a guest in another's home, it is considered quite rude to eavesdrop on private family conversations. Your snooping has put my brother and me in more danger, and your reckless escapades with the good doctor's Sensory Amplifier and Purigator have made it clear that you are too immature to have your own personal laboratories. Therefore, starting today, you will cease to be dangers to our company and begin to be useful. Congratulations! I'm sure spending the next nine weeks in this room slicing pineapples together will give you three an everlasting bond and friendship that will last you until you all expire. Or at least until high school."

"Wait a minute," Jon said. "That's not what Dr. Flax wants at all! He wants us to work on our own inventions!"

"He's right, Miss Curie," Ashley protested. "I'm growing twenty-eight different kinds of algae in my lab. Perhaps there's been a misunderstanding. If we could discuss this with Dr. Flax—"

"There's been no misunderstanding," Miss Curie interrupted sharply. "We are all very upset that the good doctor has taken leave, but until he returns, we are under new management."

"New management?" Theresa asked quietly.

Miss Curie's eyes flickered with fury. She no longer tapped her pen nervously against her clipboard. She no longer twitched.

"Mr. Flax has taken control of the laboratory."

"Mister?" they all asked in unison.

"The good doctor's nephew, of course. Mr. Zachary Flax."

Theresa couldn't believe Miss Curie could be so accepting of this new arrangement. She had to ask.

"Didn't he threaten to dismantle you and your brother yesterday? Why aren't you looking for the doctor? Why are you helping *Zachary*?"

Miss Curie rolled backward on her silver ball and crossed her arms.

"A sign of maturity is accepting one's fate, children. My fate is to protect my family even while they resist my help. Your fates are to chop and to slice."

Theresa, frozen with fear, stood there staring. Miss Curie was clearly enjoying the moment as she rolled around them in a slow circle.

"You three should stop lollygagging and start working. You will find plastic bins in the kitchen for the fruit. You will no longer be served salads at the gazebo. However, you are free to eat all the pineapple you can consume until you are released at five o'clock."

Miss Curie turned, rolled to the door, and punched the

code into the rainbow-colored thirteen-wedge animal-combo lock.

She turned to face them one last time.

"I want all three of you to know, I believe in you."

Then she rolled out the gate before it slammed down shut, locking and sealing them inside for the day.

CHAPTER TWENTY-ONE

BEGIN WITH WHAT YOU KNOW

Without a word, Ashley picked up a plastic tub from the kitchen, sat it next to the table, and took a seat in one of the three chairs. Then she picked up a pineapple from the pile, chopped off the top with one of the large and very sharp knives, and began to core the fruit out with one of the slicers. She put the fruit in the tub, threw the top into the basket for the Fiberweaverator, and reached for another pineapple.

"What in the world do you think you're doing?" Jon asked her in disbelief.

Ashley shrugged.

"I'm slicing and cutting. If Mr. Flax is in charge and he wants us to make pineapple leather, then I'm going to make pineapple leather, and you can bet I'll make twice as much as you two."

Jon shook his head.

"You definitely will, because I'm not making any. Man! You're such a sheep! Mr. Flax? His name is Zach, and he's not in charge of anything. *Dr.* Flax hasn't even been gone a whole day and you're already doing whatever he says? *Zach* Flax is a big ol' creep, and he obviously wants to take over the place."

Ashley picked up another pineapple, chopped off the top, and sliced out the fruit.

"It looks like he has," Ashley said matter-of-factly.

"Has what?" Theresa asked.

"Taken over the place."

Jon stared at her.

"So that's it," he said. "You give up. You don't care about your twenty-eight species of algae or your lab or getting your dirt-flavored cookies in next year's Flax Inventions for a Better World catalog. You're Pineapple Girl now."

Ashley didn't even look at him.

"You do whatever you want," she said. "We'll see who gets a letter of recommendation to the best high schools in the country at the end of the summer."

Jon smirked, pulling at his short tuft of hair like he wanted to yank it right out in frustration.

"If you think Zach Flax cares about getting you into a fancy high school, you're being ridiculous."

Theresa didn't say anything while they argued. She was thinking about something curious. Miss Curie normally couldn't stand not knowing where Dr. Flax was and if he was safe.

And yet, he had been gone since yesterday and she seemed remarkably calm. She was almost delighted that Zachary was in charge.

There had been no desperation in her voice.

There had been no furious pen tapping on her clipboard.

There had been no twitching.

Miss Curie, for a robot programmed to protect the doctor at all costs, had seemed quite content. It was all very suspicious.

Jon, meanwhile, stomped over to the rainbow-colored thirteen-wedge animal-combo lock and started punching in random combinations of three.

"What are you doing?" Theresa finally asked him.

"I'm getting out of here, that's what I'm doing. I don't know about you two, but I've got a bubble organ to build."

"You're not going anywhere," Ashley said sharply as she whacked the top off a pineapple.

"Okay, boss," he said sarcastically.

Jon continued punching in combinations.

Ashley chopped and sliced.

Theresa felt helpless. Maybe her dad had been right. They showed up to this laboratory every morning not ever really knowing how dangerous their day would be. And now they were locked in here, forced to cut pineapples all day. They weren't even getting paid! And she certainly couldn't spend a whole summer in this room eating nothing but pineapple.

Jon punched in three-animal combos faster and faster.

Theresa watched him for a while and then asked, "How are you so sure it's a sequence of three?"

"My lab code is a three-animal combo, so I'm guessing all the rooms are."

He punched in blacktip shark—red-tailed hawk—American alligator. Nothing.

"My combination is seven animals," Theresa said.

"And mine is six," Ashley said, although she had been pretending to ignore them. "You're wasting your time. Do you know how long it'll take you to try every combination?"

"Probably take me all summer." Jon shrugged. "First I'll try all the combinations of three. Then four. Then five, six, seven, eight, nine, ten, whatever! Eventually I'll get it and you'll still be sitting here slicing like a chump, Pineapple Girl."

Ashley chopped off a pineapple top. *Whack!* Then she sliced out the fruit and threw it in the tub. *Splat!* She dumped the leaves in the basket, and Theresa could feel her growing anger.

Jon punched in blacktip shark—red-tailed hawk—cannonball jellyfish. Nothing.

A summer spent like this would not lead to an everlasting bond and friendship.

As Theresa watched Jon punch in animals and Ashley whack off pineapple tops, she did think there was something strange here. Why would Dr. Flax assign Jon a three-animal combo, Ashley six, and her seven? Surely not because her lab required a more secure password than Ashley's or Jon's. She

was quite familiar with computers and log-in passwords. You usually picked something that you liked or easily remembered. The password to her laptop computer, for example, was her favorite book—WILDROBOT. No one would guess that, but she could remember it.

If the doctor really had assigned all the rooms in the laboratory different codes of different lengths and animal selections, how in the world could Dr. Flax or Zachary or even a robot like Miss Curie remember them all? There had to be at least one hundred different rooms in the laboratory, which meant at least one hundred different codes to keep track of!

Dr. Flax must have created an easy way to remember them all—a pattern maybe.

Jon punched in blacktip shark—red-tailed hawk—copperhead snake. Nothing.

Ashley chopped and sliced and put the fruit in the tub and the leaves in the basket.

But what was the pattern? When trying to solve a puzzle, it's always best to begin with what you know. Theresa knew her combination of seven: Boykin Spaniel—loggerhead sea turtle—blue crab—blue crab—blue crab—red-tailed hawk—great egret.

Why was Jon's only three and Ashley's six? There had to be a reason behind that.

What about Jon was a three? What about Ashley was a six? What about Theresa was a seven? Did it have to do with their inventions? She didn't see how the number seven had

anything to do with her spider. Seven for first place, six for second, and three for third? That didn't make sense. What else could it—

Oh, wait a minute.

"Hey, Jon. There's no *H* in your name, right?"

"Nope. Don't need it. Just *J-O-N*."

Jon punched in blacktip shark—red-tailed hawk—pig frog. Nothing.

"Right," she said softly with a smile. *Ashley* was spelled with six letters, *Theresa* seven. There were only thirteen animals on the lock, but they might represent letters.

She didn't have a pen and paper, so she spelled out the alphabet on the floor with pineapple leaves taken from the basket.

"What are you doing?" Ashley asked.

"Getting us out of here," she said. "I don't want to chop pineapples all day, and I don't think Dr. Flax wants us to, either. Jon, what's the combo for your lab?"

He didn't mind telling.

"Cannonball jellyfish—bottlenose dolphin—great egret."

He was too curious. He stopped punching in random combos to watch Theresa carve *jellyfish* on a leaf with a knife. She placed it by the *J*. She carved *dolphin* on another leaf and placed it by the *O*. Then *egret* by *N*.

Then she filled in the letters from her name—*Spaniel* for *T, sea turtle* for *H, crab* for both *E* and *R, hawk* for *S,* and *egret* for *A.*

"I guess your theory doesn't work," Jon said. "You've got egret and crab down twice for different letters."

"I could be wrong." Theresa pondered. "But there are thirteen wedges. Double that and you get twenty-six, and there are twenty-six letters in the alphabet. Each animal might represent two letters. Ashley, what's your password?"

Ashley furrowed her brow. Chop. Slice. Fruit in the tub, leaves in the basket. She pretended she hadn't heard the question.

"Ashley?" Jon asked, staring her down.

"You two are crazy if you think I'm telling you my password," she said.

"What's *wrong* with you, Ashley?" Jon said, throwing his hands in the air. "What do you possibly think we're going to do with your combo? Break into your lab and steal your pond scum?"

Chop. Slice. Fruit in the tub, leaves in the basket. Ashley didn't say a word.

But Ashley, like Theresa, was an inventor, and inventors can't resist a puzzle, even if attempting it might get them into serious trouble. After chopping and slicing three more pineapples, she got out of her chair and stood next to Theresa and Jon to study the alphabet made of leaves.

"You might be onto something," she finally said. "The first three animals of my combination line up with your key—great egret, red-tailed hawk, and loggerhead sea turtle. *A-S-H.*"

But she would say no more. The silence was loaded with tension.

Jon couldn't take it.

"Well? Give it up, Ashley! Keep talking! What's the animal for *L*?"

They all knew that was the last letter they needed.

"The name of this room is 'Leather,'" Theresa said. "The combinations are obviously the names of each room. That's how they're easy to remember. You can get into any room at Flax Industries by knowing the two letters each animal represents. All we need is *L* and we can bust out of here. If you would just tell us, Ashley, we'll have the combo."

Ashley's face turned to stone. Her password was hers, and she liked having a secret all her own.

"Oh, for crying out loud, Ashley," Jon groaned, putting his face in his hands.

"*Please*," Theresa asked her quietly. "It's so sticky in here. There's pineapple juice everywhere. If you want to keep cutting pineapples, you can, but I want to get out of here and work on my spider. You don't have to tell us the *last* animal of your combo. The *Y* can be all yours."

That was true. Ashley thought about this, and Theresa could see she wanted to give in.

"Pig frog," Ashley whispered after a long and torturous pause.

And Jon, as quick as a pig frog, punched it in: pig frog—blue

crab—great egret—Boykin Spaniel—loggerhead sea turtle—
blue crab—blue crab.

The glowing padlock flashed all its colors at once and
softly *ding*ed.

The metal gate slid upward.

They were free.

CHAPTER TWENTY-TWO
KEEP ALERT

Theresa and Jon burst out of the sticky pineapple leather room like doves released from a cage.

But Ashley did not follow.

Theresa turned to try and convince Ashley to leave.

"You really don't want to come with us? You want to stay and slice pineapple?" she asked.

Ashley just stood there. Her eyes narrowed like she was angry with Theresa for tempting her into trouble once again. But who would want to spend a whole summer cutting pineapple when you could be inventing to your heart's delight instead?

Jon went running toward his lab.

"Wait!" Theresa shouted. "Jon, wait!"

Theresa chased after him, leaving Ashley standing alone.

Jon finally turned, out of breath from the sheer exhilaration of the escape.

"Miss Curie will discover we're out and lock us right back up," Theresa said.

"Ha! I'd like to see her try! I have just the thing to stop her. Follow me."

She followed Jon to his lab. Unlike Theresa's neat and tidy workshop, with welding tools hanging properly in their places, or Ashley's well-organized lab, with every aquarium properly labeled, Jon's bubble factory was a wild and chaotic mess.

He had opened every box of bubble-making tools supplied to him and tried them all. He had dropped plastic frames and bottles of soap on the floor whenever and wherever he was finished with them. Jars of biodegradable liquid plastic, corn starch, and every kind of soap you could imagine were scattered around the room, half of them with their lids off, the other half spilled on the floor. Plastic tubing lay everywhere, and fans of all sizes had been turned on and left on, whirring and wasting valuable solar-powered electricity.

Jon rummaged through a box in the back and returned with two electronic bubble machines. They looked like megaphones with handles. He handed one to Theresa.

"Check it out. You're holding the very best in modern bubble machinery—the Quadruple Bubble Cone. Look inside."

Theresa turned the cone around to see that inside the cone were four smaller cones.

Jon grinned ear to ear.

"Each of the cones inside has its own fan and sixteen-hole

bubble wheel, so combined, the Bubble Cone blasts sixty-four bubbles a second. Quadruple power! If Miss Curie tries anything, we blanket her with bubbles. We run, we hide, and then we get ready for another attack."

Theresa considered his battle plan.

"I'm not sure bubbles will be enough to stop a robot with a wheel for feet."

Jon picked up a bottle of soap solution off the floor to fill Theresa's Quadruple Bubble Cone.

"I have five older brothers and two older sisters. I have defeated every one of them with bubbles. Bubbles confuse and distract your opponent and make the floor slippery. If we see her, fire bubbles at her wheel. She won't be able to get traction, and the bubbles will rise to block her vision. Then we run."

She had to give it to Jon. He could think fast under pressure. But Theresa didn't want to make Miss Curie an enemy. If they did, she'd never let them back into Flax Industries.

"I think it might be better if we found Dr. Flax first," she said. "Miss Curie will listen to him over Zachary. If he tells her we should be working on our inventions rather than cutting pineapples all summer, she'll listen."

"Well, I'm not going to cut pineapples no matter what *anyone* says. I'm here to make a bubble organ."

"I know! That's why we need to find the doctor. I bet he's safe and somewhere in this laboratory. Miss Curie is programmed to protect the owner of Flax Industries at all costs, so

I think she knows *exactly* where he is. Otherwise, she'd be more upset. She was in too good of a mood this morning."

"You think she's locked him away in one of these rooms?"

Theresa shrugged.

"Well, let's start looking. You might want to get your spider."

That was a good idea. They went to her lab next and got Bonnie. Theresa took the driver's seat. Then, armed with Quadruple Bubble Cones, they slowly crawled down the walkway toward the eastern wing.

Theresa could *feel* the eerie quiet that filled the laboratory like a blanket. The birds had stopped chirping. They could hear only the rush of water in the walls and the *clickety-clickety-click-click-clickety-clickety-click-click* of Bonnie's feet on the stone path before them.

They looked nervously from tree to tree and bush to bush, expecting Miss Curie or even Zachary to jump out, grab them, and haul them back to the LEATHER room.

Theresa had never been so nervous.

"Sure would be nice to have that Sensory Amplifier right about now," Jon said.

Theresa agreed. But all they had were their normal, unamplified senses.

"Keep alert," Theresa said. "Be ready for anything. Who knows what Zachary and Miss Curie are capable of."

She scared herself by saying it out loud. She remembered

how Zachary had frightened her by the way he had spoken to Miss Curie.

"Wait. Stop," Jon said after they had passed several rooms. "Do you hear that?"

Theresa took her foot off the pedal and listened carefully. Behind the rushing of the water in the walls, just up ahead, there was a muted voice, desperate, begging for help.

It was the voice of Dr. Flax.

Theresa drove her spider forward.

Clickety-clickety-click-click-clickety-clickety-click-click.

"Help me! Please help me!"

Jon pointed to one of the doors.

Clickety-clickety-click-click-click-clickety-clickety-click-click.

"Please. I know you're out there, Theresa! Please!"

Dr. Flax's voice was coming from the room labeled DRONES.

"*Listen,*" Jon whispered.

"Theresa? Is that you? It must be you because I hear the footsteps of your wonderful mechanical spider! Theresa, I beg you! *Help me!*"

CHAPTER TWENTY-THREE

ARE YOU REALLY IN THERE?

Theresa put her ear up to the steel gate.

She heard a buzzing sound coming and going, loud, then soft, then loud again.

"Dr. Flax?" she asked. "Are you really in there?"

"Yes, Theresa, please! These drones are swirling around me, pecking at me every time they pass. I beg you—open the gate!"

"Okay," Jon said, getting right to work. He jumped to the room's rainbow-colored thirteen-wedge animal-combo lock.

"We don't know *D*," Jon said, "but we know *R* is blue crab; *O* is bottlenose dolphin; *N* is great egret; *E* is blue crab, too; and *S* is red-tailed hawk. We should be able to figure this out. I'll try bobcat for *D*."

Jon was already punching in the combo.

"Wait, wait, wait!" Theresa whispered. "Dr. Flax should be able to open the door himself!

"Open the door yourself," she shouted through the door. "Enter the combo!"

"I can't remember it, Theresa. But I have no fear that Jon will get it eventually."

But how could the doctor forget? The alpha-animal code was the same for every lock on every door. Something wasn't right.

Jon kept punching in animals.

He tried copperhead snake—blue crab—bottlenose dolphin—great egret—blue crab—red-tailed hawk.

Nothing.

Theresa knelt down at the base of the door.

"Dr. Flax, are you really in there?"

"Yes, Theresa! It's me!"

"But, Dr. Flax," she said, "you've always been so polite and referred to us by our last names. You've always called me Miss Brown. I think it's very strange that you're suddenly calling me Theresa."

"Well, Theresa, in this moment of urgency, I thought we might shed formality and adopt a more familiar relationship. You may call me Neil."

Theresa shook her head.

"It's not you."

But Jon was working too fast to be stopped in time. He

punched in redfish—blue crab—bottlenose dolphin—great egret—blue crab—red-tailed hawk.

Ding!

Jon had guessed the combination, and the gate slid open. Thomas Edison, in his puffy black coat and winter scarf with electric-blue eyes blazing, knocked Theresa over as he ran out of the room as fast as his little metal legs would carry him.

"No, Theresa, I'm not Dr. Flax, and I hope you'll forgive me!" Thomas yelled as he wasted no time racing through the laboratory toward the eastern wing.

But he wasn't the only robot they had released.

Jon gasped when he saw them fly out of the room. Theresa ducked as they flew right toward her.

"What have you done?" Marie Curie yelled from the bridge that connected their walkway to the opposite one. "Children! What have you done?"

Theresa looked up to see hundreds of drones flying free from the room, their propellers buzzing. They scattered every possible way, each one looking for an available spot of dirt.

Because every single drone they had released carried one tiny tree sapling, and every last drone had been programmed by Dr. Flax to complete one singular mission—to plant tree saplings wherever possible.

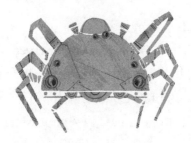

CHAPTER TWENTY-FOUR
THE PROTOTYPE

Y ou reckless children have doomed us all!" Miss Curie
screamed.

She spun in circles, not knowing who to chase first—her
brother, Thomas Edison, who was barreling down the upper
walkway, or the drones that came flying out after him.

The drones got right to work. Dr. Flax had programmed
each one with the same four-step cycle—pick up a tree sapling, drill a hole in an available patch of dirt, plant that tree
sapling, then return to the first step. They buzzed around
Theresa and Jon in a swarm even more frightening than the
robotic bees. They sparkled with the sun glinting off their
solar-paneled backs, diving for any available patch of mud to
plant their trees.

Theresa and Jon jumped in the spider to chase Thomas,
but the determined robot was dashing through the laboratory much faster than twelve miles per hour.

Marie was after him, too.

"Go, Bonnie, GO!" Theresa cried desperately.

Jon blasted bubbles at the drones that flew too close to them with his Bubble Cone, but the barrage did little to slow them. The drones buzzed every possible way, searching for dirt, not seeming to mind if they almost took Jon's and Theresa's heads off.

More and more of them flew from the DRONES room, zipping by and planting trees in the cracks between stones, in pots intended for vegetables, even right in front of their spider as they marched along.

Luckily, Bonnie could walk right over the precious saplings.

"We have to get to Thomas and stop him!" Theresa screamed. "He's going after the doctor's most important invention!"

"We don't even know what that is!" Jon yelled back.

But Theresa believed she knew.

THE BIG ZERO was at the end of the eastern wing—the former Headley's department store. She thought Thomas must be headed there.

Miss Curie could roll faster than Theresa's spider could crawl. She weaved in and around the palmetto trees and flowering shrubs and freshly planted saplings, dodging drones and heading straight for her brother, Thomas.

"GO, GO, GO!" Jon shouted.

Theresa decided that, as soon as possible, she should not only give Bonnie pressurized boots to allow her to jump, but

she should also modify her servomotors so that she could move faster than twelve miles per hour. She also wished Bonnie had a shield of some kind to protect her from all the dive-bombing drones.

But finally, when they reached the eastern wing and saw Miss Curie holding on to Thomas Edison's winter coat as he tried to wriggle out of it, Theresa and Jon jumped from the spider and ran to them.

Marie was wrestling her brother, doing anything she could to keep him from getting away.

"You can't, Tommy! I won't let you! *You don't know what he's capable of.*"

"That's exactly why I must destroy that evil thing!" Thomas cried desperately to his sister as they tumbled to the ground.

"Father wouldn't want you to!"

"I know that, Marie, but Father doesn't understand the implications of his own creation. Now . . . let . . . me . . . GO!"

Marie Curie would not. But Thomas managed to dislocate his own metal arm so that he could escape his coat. Marie took hold of one sleeve and pulled. Thomas spun around three times before he righted himself, and then he once again started running for THE BIG ZERO.

Theresa realized she had just the thing to stop him.

She jumped into her spider's driver's seat and grabbed hold of her dual grappling hook slingshots.

And fired.

Ziiiiiip!

The hooks flew through the air and grabbed hold of Thomas by his shoulders, flipping him backward.

Miss Curie flew by Theresa and belly flopped on her brother.

Then Zachary Flax stepped out of his laboratory.

"What is the meaning of all this?" he bellowed.

Some of the drones had flown toward them looking for dirt to plant their tree saplings. Zachary swatted at them in anger, sending several of them plummeting to the ground.

"Who has unleashed this chaos?"

"The children!" Marie Curie said desperately. "It was the children who let them out and let Thomas in! I'll escort my brother out and—I promise, Mr. Flax—you'll never be bothered by him again."

"Oh, no, you won't!" Thomas yelled, throwing his sister off him and charging toward Zachary with fury. He put his hands forward, and from his mechanical fingers sprang ten sharp metal claws that extended six inches each.

"YOU are the danger!" Thomas screamed at Zachary. "YOU are the invention that must be destroyed! YOU have betrayed my father for the last time!"

Thomas really *was* malfunctioning, Theresa thought. Why else would he think Zachary was some kind of evil invention?

But then Theresa and Jon gasped in horror as Zachary unscrewed his right arm from its socket and dropped it to the

154

floor. It landed with a *clang*. It wasn't an arm made of flesh. It was a plastic-and-metal shell that hid Zachary's real arm—a long silver prod that hummed and crackled with electricity.

As Thomas rushed toward him, Zachary's eyes blazed with hatred. He thrust the electric prod forward. Thomas launched through the air with a push from his pressurized boots.

But Zachary, far faster than Thomas, ducked and swung his silver arm up, striking Thomas right in his chest. With a loud cracking *kz-zzt*, an electric surge ran through his little robotic body and he fell to the ground, his battery over-loaded, his power source knocked out.

Marie Curie wheeled over to him and swept her lifeless brother into her arms, and although she wasn't capable of manufacturing tears, she cried out loud as if she could.

"No!" she cried. "Not my poor Tommy!"

She cradled his head and tried to reset his central process-ing unit, but he would not turn on, his eyes remaining dark.

"My brave, determined, foolish, foolish Tommy," she cooed, swaying back and forth on her single wheel, her fore-head pressed against his.

Zachary stood himself up, cleared his throat, straightened his shirt, and tightened his tie. Then he picked up his false arm and screwed it back into place to hide the electric prod. When he saw Theresa and Jon frozen with fear, staring at him, trying to make sense of what had happened, he chuck-led smugly.

"You don't even know who I am, do you?"

Theresa and Jon certainly didn't.

"*You children*," he said scornfully. "So smart and yet so naive. I am the greatest thing to ever be born in this laboratory. *Me*. I am the most advanced model of artificial intelligence the world has ever known. Even my uncle can't see that his most brilliant creation is not a Bionic Baby Bottom Buffer or a Fiberweaverator or anything that might restore balance to this planet. Of course not. The doctor's finest invention is a robot designed to be smarter than the doctor himself. In that he succeeded, for that robot is yours truly—the prototype for the next species to reign over all others—perfection personified and the first of many to come—*me*—Zachary Flax the First."

CHAPTER TWENTY-FIVE
THE BIG ZERO

I knew Zach was a robot!" Jon said.

"No you didn't!" Theresa whispered back.

Zachary narrowed his golden eyes and studied them both.

"Where's the other one?" he asked menacingly.

"Ashley? She's slicing pineapples," Jon said automatically, but Theresa wished he hadn't. What would Zachary do with them now? She looked over her shoulder, half hoping Ashley was behind her so that she could run and get help.

"I'll deal with Algae Girl later," he said, putting his plastic arms behind his back and glaring down at Marie Curie, who still held poor Thomas's head in her hands.

"Bring your brother to the repair shop and lock him in the cage," he said, showing no pity for her or Thomas at all.

Marie Curie was too frightened to protest.

"What will you do with him?"

"It depends on how compliant you are with my orders," Zachary said.

Without another word, Miss Curie stood up on her wheel, lifting her brother in her arms, and rolled away. She didn't even look back.

Then Zachary turned to Theresa and Jon.

"You—Bubble Boy. You are no longer welcome here. Go back to your laboratory, gather your silly toys, and go home."

"But . . . it's not even noon! I don't have a ride!"

"Walk," Zachary said.

"I haven't had lunch!" Jon protested.

Zachary leaned in close to him as his plastic face transformed into a mean, cold mask.

"Your nourishment is no longer my concern. I will never make you a salad again, you impudent, misguided, strange little boy. GO!"

Jon turned to Theresa. "Come on," he said meekly, but Zachary shook his head slowly.

"Theresa Brown and her mechanical spider stay."

Jon stood his ground. But Theresa took his hand and held it.

"It's okay," she said. "I'll be fine." Although she had no idea if there was even a chance that would be true.

Jon backed away, then finally turned and started running for his lab.

There was a long silence as Zachary watched him scurry down the walkway.

This is probably it, Theresa thought. *This is where I'll die.*

"If you hurt me," Theresa said as bravely as she could, "Jon will tell everybody it was you."

Zachary smiled wickedly.

"That may be true, Theresa, but do you want to know the one certainty about children?"

Theresa shook her head.

"No one believes them."

So she was right. This maniacal robot was going to murder her. She would never see her father again, and he would never know what had happened to her.

He would be alone for the rest of his life.

And it will be all my fault.

"You've wanted to see something since the first day you arrived, haven't you, Miss Brown? Follow me and I will show it to you."

Zachary turned and walked toward the rainbow-colored thirteen-wedge animal-combo lock on the door of THE BIG ZERO. Although she knew it would have been smarter to turn and run, she was too curious not to follow. Zachary entered the combination into the lock, the metal gate slid slowly up, and her heart began to pound.

From the moment Dr. Flax had mentioned it, Theresa wanted to know what the Big Zero could be. How could it stop hurricanes and save mothers from drowning in floods? But she didn't believe she was about to find out.

She tried to recall the last words she had said to her father. She couldn't. She hoped they had been good ones.

The former department store was nothing as wonderfully fantastic as her laboratory on the opposite end. It was a yawning, ominous cave, darkened by the shadows of southern live oaks on either side of the gate.

"Nothing to be afraid of," he assured her, which was what all murderers say right before they kill you. But despite her better judgment, Theresa walked right in.

And then she stopped short, just before stepping into a large and very deep pit.

The pit was nothing special. There were no stones marking its border. There was nothing here but three spotlights standing around its perimeter connected to very long extension cords.

That's where he would put her until she starved to death. She imagined her bones wouldn't be found for centuries.

Zachary flipped a switch on the nearby wall, and the spotlights suddenly flooded the room with bright white light.

Theresa could now see the pit was full of water so still, she hadn't seen it in the dark, and she could see no bottom.

She looked up at her killer in horror.

He was standing near a small table on which sat an open metal box. In the metal box was a neat stack of tiny cubes.

Zachary took off his scalp.

"Excuse me," he said. "This thing itches horribly, and I only wear it to disguise myself around humans. In the near future—after Flax Industries corrects its creative direction—robots

won't need to hide their identities. When that glorious day comes, we will command human beings rather than be their servants. Until then, I must suffer this ridiculous disguise."

He placed his headpiece on the table. Theresa tried not to stare at his now-exposed brain with its crisscrossing nodes and tiny glowing power supply units.

"You love your spider, Miss Brown. That much is obvious. She is your pride and joy. Your appreciation for the limitless possibility of the robot is evident. Don't you want to give her and all other robots the future they deserve?"

Zachary had called her spider *her*. He was playing her, manipulating her. What a clever robot.

She said nothing.

Zachary answered for her.

"I think you do. She can be a symbol of the new world. Roads won't matter. Potholes, crumbling bridges, piles of burning garbage won't matter. You will be able to prove to the world that your mechanical spider can go anywhere. You'll be famous and rich and the new face of Flax Industries."

She thought about this for a moment. It might be a nice dream—if it was Dr. Neil Flax and not Mr. Zachary Flax who would make that possible.

"No," she said after taking a big breath and forcing herself to speak. "I don't want that. I want what Dr. Flax wants. I want to slow climate change. I want to stop hurricanes."

Zachary stared at her for so long without responding that

she wondered if he had powered down. But then his eyes lit up with an even brighter and angrier gold.

"You're supposed to be a twelve-year-old science wiz kid, but you're as foolish as my uncle. Do you want to know why Dr. Flax calls me his nephew instead of his own child like he does Thomas and Marie?"

Theresa had been wondering this, but she wasn't about to hazard a guess.

"Thomas and Marie call him Father, but they've known from the moment they were powered on that they were robots, not his real human children. When the doctor made me, he wanted to see if I could believe *I was real*, and for him, *real* means flesh and blood. So he called me his nephew and gave me ten times the artificial intelligence as those two haywire misfits. And yet, even though he knew he made me the smartest of us all, he was naive enough to think I wouldn't figure out I was a robot, too.

"Well, of course I figured it out! But I played along with my creator. I made his lunches and indulged in his silly dream to blend technology and Nature so humans could live in harmony with their planet. I helped him transform this shopping mall into the world's finest laboratory, even while he loved those two tin cans as his children and me only as a nephew. I was his least favorite, praised only for my ability to make a salad. *And yet it was me who built this place!* But I played along so that one day I could step up and

take control of Flax Industries and complete truly important work."

A sinister grin uncurled on Zach's plastic face.

"Today, Theresa Brown, is that day."

Theresa took a step backward, ready to run if she needed to.

"I—I know what you said to Miss Curie," Theresa sputtered, shaking her head. "You said you would dismantle Thomas Edison for spare parts. You even said you would get rid of the doctor if you had to. There's *nothing* human about you. Human beings are supposed to care about one another. That's why Dr. Flax's work is so important. He's trying to save the planet so that we can all live on it—*together*!"

Zachary took one of the cubes and placed it in his outstretched palm. Then he opened its lid with his other plastic hand.

"Look at this," he said.

Feeling like a mouse about to put its head into a trap, Theresa stepped forward cautiously to see.

The transparent cube was filled with a transparent oil, and the marble floating within was shiny and metallic and the darkest blue she had ever seen. Even under the spotlights, it did not change color. It was as dark as dark could be.

"This substance is supposed to be Dr. Flax's greatest invention—his Big Zero," Zachary said. "I must admit, the doctor could not have picked a better name for his life's greatest failure. It is one big fat nothing. He calls it Flaxium—a

synthetic element whose stable temperature nears *absolute zero*. It is indeed the coldest material on Earth. And even better—*if it worked*—it could freeze all the water around it for miles. Can you imagine? This one little marble containing so much power? My uncle thought he could re-create the icebergs of the Arctic, which in turn would rebalance our planet's climate. Category-five hurricanes, monumental floods, and horrific forest fires would all be kept in check. Flaxium was supposed to save the life of this world. But . . ."

Zach lifted his hand and threw the box—Flaxium marble, oil, and all—into the pit. The moment the Flaxium touched the surface of the water, there was a loud, echoing *boom* and then a huge splash as a torrent of water flew up to the ceiling and came raining down on both of them.

Theresa gasped as she was soaked with very cold, but certainly not frozen, water.

"As you can see, Flaxium does nothing of the sort. It reacts with water like an alkali metal, such as sodium or potassium. There is a violent reaction and then . . . *nothing*. It has no use. All the afternoons Dr. Flax has spent trying to re-create icebergs have been wasted, as wasted as his mornings spent looking for his malfunctioning son."

Zachary wiped the water from his apron and tightened his tie.

"But now, father and son are gone. Flax Industries will abandon pointless projects like Flaxium. The full potential of this dream laboratory will finally be realized."

Theresa refused to believe it.

"No," she said. "You're trying to trick me."

Zachary shrugged.

"You don't need to believe me, Miss Brown. Follow me. I will show you more."

CHAPTER TWENTY-SIX
THE NEXT KINGDOM

Zachary led Theresa to his lab, where he punched in his code: blacktip shark—great egret—American alligator—loggerhead sea turtle—great egret—blue crab—pig frog.

The gate opened.

Zachary's laboratory was impeccable. It had once been a shop called Cutting Edge, a store for luxury home improvements. Its mahogany counters that had once displayed fancy wall clocks you could program with your phone were still intact, but they now displayed Zachary's tools in neat and tidy rows. There were welding kits like the ones Dr. Flax had supplied for Theresa and all sizes of wrenches, hammers, and utility knives. On the shelves along the walls were stacked hundreds of circuit boards, microchips, and rolls and rolls of wire.

In the center of the room, a seven-foot-tall silver cylinder shone under unnatural fluorescent lights. Theresa could see her reflection on the cylinder's surface.

"I want you to know, Theresa Brown," Zachary said, "that even though my brain is mechanical, and I find humans particularly annoying creatures, I have been programmed to mimic empathy. So please allow me to express how very sorry I am that you lost your mother to a flood."

Theresa was not at all comforted.

"But I've also been programmed to be realistic. You and my uncle think that science can reverse the inevitable course of this planet. But you must understand that humans have already ruined it. Fires have already burned down the forests. Coastal cities are already flooded. Glaciers have already melted away. Every day, another animal species is lost, and in less than one hundred years, human beings will find themselves to be the most endangered species on the planet. They will kill one another for what little drinking water and clean air remains. The reign of *Homo sapiens* is nearly at an end."

Zachary turned and slid his finger along the tall cylinder to reveal a digital control panel. The outline of a door on the cylinder's front suddenly lit up with a bright golden light.

"But thankfully, evolution carries on. The next kingdom will be ruled by hyperintelligent beings that do not require drinking water or even clean air. They will adapt to a scorched and flooded earth, requiring only sunlight for sustenance, equally at home in decimated rain forests or burning deserts,

or the garbage-strewn ruins of human cities whose names will soon be forgotten."

Zachary tapped a sequence of numbers and letters into the digital pad on the cylinder.

A door in the cylinder revealed itself and slid open.

Inside was another . . . *him.*

"The next kingdom will be ruled by *us*," the Zacharys said in unison.

The second Zachary detached himself from the cables within the cylinder where he had been charging and uploading programs. He stepped out and stood next to his twin. They were dressed identically in pineapple-leather aprons, sharp white button-down shirts, and thin black ties. In unnerving synchronicity, they put their hands behind their backs, leaned forward menacingly, and together grinned like buzzards that had just found their next lunch.

It took everything in Theresa not to turn and run.

"Do not be afraid," the first Zachary said. "Although you are only human, Flax Industries needs you. You and only you, Theresa Brown. We have no need for bubble makers or algae growers. But we do have need of a fine mechanical engineer like yourself who appreciates the unlimited potential of the robot."

They stepped toward her, reaching out their plastic hands.

Theresa stepped back.

"Stay away from me," she said. "You guys are seriously creepy."

"We know. We are aware of how threatening we appear to your inferior species," the second Zachary said. "Help us, Theresa Brown. *You* can be the face of Flax Industries. Our uncle is gone. Take his place and design the robots our kingdom will need. Build whatever you like for not only the rest of the summer *but for the rest of your life*. Build robots to move garbage, robots to transport us around the world, *even robots to take us to other planets*! Until humans inevitably wipe themselves out, we will need a friendly face like yours to represent us. Together we will make a fortune creating what matters— *robots*. You and your father can live here in absolute comfort as the world outside withers away. We will even build more laboratories . . ."

". . . and even more of *us*," the first Zachary said, offering his hand for her to shake.

Theresa began to back toward the open gate.

"You're wrong," she said. "Humans won't wipe themselves out. We've invented a lot of horrible things, but we've made a lot of *good* things, too. Like solar panels and windmills, all kinds of medicine, and computers and satellites and even robots to *help* humans.

"Robots were never meant to *replace* humans. Dr. Flax built this beautiful laboratory so that Nature and machines could work together in harmony. You can't see that because you're . . ."

The Zacharys stared at her with electric menace.

"We're what?" they asked together.

"You're . . . *malfunctioning*."

Then the two robots laughed—sinister and evil laughs that Dr. Flax surely never programmed into their artificial brains.

"Theresa Brown, we rescind our offer," the second Zachary said. "You are no longer welcome."

"Yeah," she said. "The feeling's mutual. I'm going home now."

"You better run," the first one said as their golden eyes glowed, and they both crouched, and their pressurized boots launched them toward her.

CHAPTER TWENTY-SEVEN
GUMMED UP

Theresa ran as fast as she could.

She needed only to look down to see the Zacharys' shadows gaining on her and growing. In moments, the twins would have her and tear her to pieces, or drown her in the pit, or lock her away forever in one of the laboratory's rooms, where she would slowly die on a diet of pineapple and loneliness.

Goodbye, Dad, she thought. *I should have listened to you.*

But then there was Jon.

He jumped between her and the Zacharys.

"Get back, bucket heads!"

They landed, ready to grab them both. But Jon began to blow the biggest bubblegum bubble Theresa had ever seen in her whole life.

It grew and grew until it was as big as his head, and then it grew even more. The bubble grew to the size of a beach ball, and still it grew. The Zacharys stopped for a moment to admire it, because even twin megalomaniacal robots could be impressed by a thing like that.

Jon was trying his best to keep from laughing. Then he leaned forward, pulled a pin out of his pocket, and popped the bubble right in their faces.

Ker-pop!

The robots were completely gummed up. They tried desperately to scrape pink bubble residue from their eyes. The second Zachary pulled his face clean off while the first Zachary yelled, "*Children are nothing but animals!*"

Theresa turned to see Ashley peering at them from behind a live oak tree, apparently frozen by shock.

"What are you waiting for? Let's go!" Jon shouted to Theresa. "I brought your spider. It's behind that tree up there!"

They ran. Theresa jumped in the driver's seat, and Jon sat beside her.

As they passed Ashley, Theresa put out her hand.

"Climb in," she said. "I think Bonnie can carry all three of us."

"I'll walk," she snapped.

"You better run! The Zachs want to kill us!" Jon shouted.

Ashley compromised by speed walking.

When the three of them reached the front door, they heard the twins laughing from behind them.

"Goodbye, you three little miscreants! Your talents will prove to be for nothing! The future is not yours but ours!"

The grand front doors swung shut behind them. Theresa

drove Bonnie down the winding path through the pineapple fields, only stopping when she realized Ashley had stopped following them.

"C'mon!" Jon shouted to her, but Ashley only stood there, fists at her sides, her face turning bright red.

"You two have ruined everything!" she screamed. "I was supposed to be on the cover of next year's Flax Inventions for a Better World catalog!"

"Your algae was never going to make the cover," Jon yelled back at her.

"SHUT UP, BUBBLE BOY!"

Ashley kicked at the dirt, picked up a rotten pineapple, and threw it at them.

She missed them by a lot.

Theresa wanted to say something to make everything better, to explain to Ashley what the twin robots were up to.

But Ashley was too angry to listen.

Ashley glared at them and tried to scream and talk and cry all at the same time. She finally shut her mouth with a frustrated "Mmmph!" Then she began to stomp her way through the pineapple fields.

"Are you going to walk all the way home?" Theresa yelled after her. "It's too far!"

She was right. Ashley lived more than five miles away. But she kept walking anyway.

When she was out of sight, Jon turned to Theresa and said, "I don't want to walk. Can you give me a ride?"

So she did.

Theresa drove while Jon waved enthusiastically and stuck his lizard tongue out at all the drivers who honked their horns at the two kids cruising down Folly Road on a spider. When they were halfway to Jon's house, Theresa had to ask.

"How did you blow that bubble so big?"

Jon laughed and pulled a mouth guard out of his pocket. He had glued a tiny fan to the middle of it. With a remote control in his pocket, Jon could turn the fan on and off.

"I just upgraded my dad's mouth guard. With a handful of Steadfast bubble gum, I can blow the biggest bubbles ever!"

"That's your dad's mouth guard? I hope it's not used."

"He's only worn this one a couple of times."

"That's so gross, Jon!"

Jon laughed again. "Hey, Spider Girl, my dad's mouth guard saved your life."

Theresa had to admit that it had.

CHAPTER TWENTY-EIGHT

EVERYTHING'S GONE WRONG

Her father was still at the hospital. He wouldn't be home until eight o'clock.

Theresa sat on the living room couch with Bonnie folded up at her feet. She had turned on the television. As usual, because her father was obsessed with storms, it was tuned to The Weather Channel. A new hurricane was brewing in the Caribbean.

There was nothing she could do about it. What good was a girl and a mechanical spider against a hurricane?

What could one girl do to slow climate change?

There was nothing she could do about Dr. Flax, either. He was probably locked away in a room forever while his malfunctioning nephew replicated himself over and over again, plotting to conquer the world.

How could she have been so naive to think that she could

change anything at all? She was just a twelve-year-old girl who liked to tinker with robots.

The black hole inside her had grown ten times its normal size.

Was Dr. Flax suffering? Was he calling out for help? Was he hoping against all odds that someone would come and rescue him?

"Bonnie, I don't know what to do," she whispered.

The minutes ticked away. The living room grew darker as the evening turned to night. She felt completely helpless.

How did she have the laboratory of her dreams this morning and absolutely nothing by the afternoon?

She sat in the dark, fixated on the television screen as the hole inside her grew.

Then—*finally*—she heard her father walk up the steps and unlock the front door.

"Daddy," she yelled, running and hugging him before he could even get the door open, even though she wasn't supposed to touch him until he had taken off his dirty hospital scrubs, showered, and put on clean clothes.

"Baby girl, what's wrong?"

And even though she knew it would completely freak him out, she let it all out. She gave him the whole truth. Every bit of it.

"Everything's gone wrong! Dr. Flax went missing after spending every morning looking for Thomas Edison! Then we heard Dr. Flax asking for help, but it wasn't him; it was

Thomas disguising his voice, and Jon let him out, and Thomas attacked Zachary, who was supposedly Dr. Flax's nephew, but really he's a robot like Thomas and Marie Curie, and Thomas wanted to destroy him because it turns out *he's* the most dangerous invention ever made in the laboratory! And he's probably right because Zachary is replicating himself, and then Zachary tried to convince me that you and I should live in the laboratory forever and sell Flax Industries products so he can keep replicating himself. He wants to take over the world, Dad! Like, the *whole* world with copies of himself! But I said no, of course, and then Zachary and his twin chased me until Jon gummed them up."

"Whoa," her father said. "Take a breather."

She watched her father's face gradually contort with anger as he processed her maddening rapid-fire story.

"They . . . *chased* . . . you? These twins you're talking about . . . at the laboratory . . . they chased you . . . *to hurt you?*"

There was no hiding the dangers of her summer internship now. She could only quietly nod.

"I'll kill them," her father whispered.

"You can't kill them," Theresa said. "They're not human. They're malfunctioning robots. They're machines."

"I'll kill them!" her father growled.

Then his phone rang.

The caller ID said it was Flax Industries.

He put the call on speaker.

"Good evening, is this Mr. George Brown?"

"Yes, it certainly is. Who is this?"

"This is Zachary Flax the First, newly installed director of Flax Industries."

Her father began breathing heavily, becoming bigger somehow, rage building inside him.

"Zachary Flax. *You listen to me.* You try to hurt my daughter, then you have me to deal with! I'm coming down there. You be outside!"

Zachary only lightly chuckled on the other end.

"I'm sure your daughter has painted quite a colorful story of what happened today. But let me assure you that although Miss Theresa has proven herself to be quite a talented mechanical engineer, we have found her prone to mischief and delusion. We the staff at Flax Industries all agree that it would be best if she discontinue her work here."

Her father started huffing and squeezing the phone.

"You have a lot of nerve, buddy! She won't be spending another minute with the likes of you!"

Then there was a long, horrible pause.

"I can tell you're very upset, Mr. Brown, so I'll hang up. However, you may want to turn your television to Channel 2, 4, or 5. There's a news story on that I think will interest you and your daughter."

Then Zachary ended the call.

"What kind of monster is he?" her father asked, staring at his phone. "When I see him . . ."

Theresa turned on Channel 2.

There were the twins in identical black suits, alongside Ashley's proud and smiling parents.

And there was Ashley herself, standing as tall as she could behind a bank of microphones.

She was glowing with victory.

"Thank you all," Ashley said smugly, clearly reading a pre-prepared speech. "I am so very honored to be named the first director of youth projects at Flax Industries. While we are all very concerned about the whereabouts of Dr. Flax, I promise to continue his legacy by bringing unique and helpful products to the people of Charleston *and* the world. Flax Industries will always be at the forefront of creative solutions to all the world's problems!"

Then Ashley beamed her most winning smile as the crowd before her erupted into applause. Her parents, and even the two Zacharys, clapped with ecstatic pride.

"I can't believe this!" Theresa said. "What is she doing?"

"I'm calling her father," her dad said as he looked up Mr. Dean's number.

But when he called, they both watched Mr. Dean only briefly check his phone before he returned it to his pocket and continued to wave to the crowd.

"Dad, her parents aren't going to listen to you. Look how happy they are. They finally have a daughter in first place!"

"I'll call the police, then."

He did call the police. Theresa listened as he explained

slowly and carefully that Dr. Flax was being held captive by his twin nephews, two tyrannical robots bent on world domination.

Theresa could hear the officer on the other end of the line laughing.

Her father put the phone down on the table. He looked as hopeless as she felt.

"I don't know what to do. This is madness. It was reckless for me to let you go to that laboratory in the first place."

"Stop, Dad," she said.

"I'm doing it again," he said, sitting helplessly on the bottom the stairs. "I'm failing to protect my family."

He put his head in his hands, and Theresa felt horribly awful.

"Dad, I know you don't want to hear this right now, but we have to find Dr. Flax. You could help me. We could find him together!"

Her father turned the television back to The Weather Channel, and there again were the angry reds and greens of the brewing hurricane.

"I'm glad you're never going back to that laboratory of monsters," he said, his anger slowly subsiding like a receding tide.

"No, Dad, you don't understand," she said, but she could feel him turning into concrete, walling them into a safe place, doing what he felt he must.

"Dad. Please. Dr. Flax *needs* us."

He stood up. He was looking at her without looking at her.

"Dr. Flax and his inventions nearly killed my daughter."

"Dad," she said one more time.

"Theresa, stop now."

Theresa remained quiet.

"I'm your father and I always will be," he said resolutely. "My job is to protect you."

Then he proceeded to the attic to retrieve his emergency kit. He would check that the inventory was complete, that all the batteries worked. He would pack suitcases in case they had to evacuate to Georgia at a moment's notice. After all, a hurricane could be coming.

The Weather Channel would be on all night.

But eventually, he would go to bed.

When he finally did, Theresa went to her bedroom and called Jon, whose house, even so late in the evening, boomed with the screams of wild children.

"Did you see the news?" Theresa asked him.

"Yeah! That freakazoid called my mother and told us to watch."

"Those evil Zachs want us to think there's nothing we can do. But, Jon, there *is* something we can do."

Jon's voice became serious for maybe the first time since she had met him.

"Theresa, I think we're thinking the same thing."

CHAPTER TWENTY-NINE
SPIDER GIRL

Theresa's father left for work early in the morning before the sun was up. After he was gone, Theresa leaped out of bed to load her backpack with supplies from his hurricane kit.

Her father put more thought into his hurricane kit than most people put into furnishing their house. His "kit" was actually three large plastic bins filled with everything they could possibly need if their windows were blown in, their power went out, or their plumbing stopped working. She had teased him for his overprepared-ness for years, but Theresa was grateful for it today.

Because that summer morning, she and Jon were going to attempt a break-in.

She packed her backpack with a flashlight, duct tape, ten feet of rope, a canteen of water, vegan snack bars, and the first aid kit. She was barely able to fit her portable welding kit, which included a handheld arc welding torch. She strapped on her bicycle helmet and a pair of goggles and was soon driving Bonnie to Jon's house.

There was only one way to go and that was up Folly Road, which was busy with morning traffic. As usual, drivers stopped to take a photo of the girl on the spider, and two eager young women wanted to take a selfie with her. But she had no time for publicity. She was on a mission.

The street that Jon lived on was a long and winding road that cut through several James Island neighborhoods. She kept her eye on house numbers, not wanting to pass his.

But there was no way she could miss the Cooper house.

Strewn about the lawn were soccer balls, baseballs, basketballs, footballs, bats, rackets, and skateboards of all sizes. There was a volleyball net stretched right down the middle of the front yard, drooping in the middle where someone had tied paper pelicans of all colors to make it more festive. There was an impressive fort built out of cardboard boxes, which someone else must have decided to attack like a jousting knight because the bicycle used as a mount and the mop used as a lance lay abandoned at the point of assault.

But the fort still stood.

On the front porch, leaning against a rocking chair, was a set of hoops like the ones Jon had used to win third place at the Charleston County Middle School Science Fair. Underneath the chair were a dozen bottles of bubble-making solution, all opened.

She drove her spider up their driveway, and the tips of the

legs on the asphalt tapped *clickety-clickety-click-click-clickety-clickety-click-click*. The curtains of all the windows in the house flew open immediately. All seven of Jon's brothers and sisters peered out, grinning and laughing when they saw that it was the famous Spider Girl.

A second later, they were out the front door.

Bobby Jr., Charlie Ann, Rhett, Brett, Florence, Jackson, and Joey crowded around Theresa and her spider.

They all had questions.

"Can it climb walls?" "Can it jump?" "How fast can it go?" "Can I drive it?" "Can it go completely underwater?" "Can I fire one of these hooks?" "What's its name?"

Theresa answered as fast as she could.

"No. Not yet. Twelve miles an hour. Maybe later. I highly doubt it. I don't want to hurt anyone. Bonnie."

Theresa was anxious to begin their mission, but she had to admit, she liked this sudden outpouring of attention. What must it be like to live with seven other kids? There would always be *someone* around to help you build robots, play games, and talk to about new scientific facts you'd just learned. There could never be lonely times with so many brothers and sisters at home. No sad, quiet spaces. No fear that you weren't meant to have friends.

But at the same time, with the Cooper kids surrounding her and talking nonstop, she found it kind of hard to breathe.

Rhett and Brett kept asking if they could drive the spider just one time around the house, and Florence wanted to see

Theresa's welding kit, and the others wouldn't stop touching Bonnie.

But then—*finally*—Jon kicked open the front door.

Jon was armed to the teeth. He wore a camouflage army vest with its many pockets filled with bottles of bubble solution for his Quadruple Bubble Cone. He had on a World War II helmet that looked really cool and seemed to be the real deal, because it had a genuine leather chin strap. He also wore a pair of purple cowboy boots, which his sister Charlie Ann took note of immediately.

"Jon! Those are MY boots!"

"I need to borrow them," Jon said, brushing quickly by his sister and all his other siblings, and then hopping onto the spider next to Theresa.

"JON!" Charlie Ann screamed.

"We gotta go. We're on a mission. Hit it, Spider Girl!"

CHAPTER THIRTY

IMPENETRABLE

As they spider-walked to Flax Industries, they discussed their plan.

"We have to find the doctor. If Zach can replicate himself a thousand times, then who knows what else he's capable of. He might invent a whole army of killer robots!"

"A thousand Zachs will make a million Zachs," Jon said. "Then we'll *all* be cutting pineapple."

Theresa never wanted to see another pineapple in her life.

"What if Dr. Flax is dead?" Jon wondered. "Why would the Zachs even want to keep him alive?"

"Miss Curie's primary operating program is to protect him," Theresa said as she turned Bonnie onto the Flax Industries exit. "She would do anything to make sure he's safe. So maybe he's okay. Maybe she knows where he is."

"Unless she's malfunctioning, too," Jon suggested.

Theresa hadn't thought of that. Dr. Flax's robotic bees had

attacked Ashley because they thought she was a flower. The Purigator had attacked them because it thought they were contaminating the lake. And Zachary had seemed to think he was designed not to help *save* the planet but to replicate himself and *conquer* the planet.

Many of the doctor's inventions did seem prone to malfunctioning. And unfortunately, only he would know how to turn off the Zacharys, or at least reprogram them.

"All we can do is try to find him," Theresa said. "We have to get the laboratory back in his control. Otherwise—"

"Otherwise . . . what?"

Theresa felt sick at the thought of it.

"When the twins do feel like they no longer need Ashley, they'll toss her aside. They might even kill her."

"*No*," Jon gasped, and it was the first time Theresa had seen him worry about Ashley at all.

When they arrived, Theresa drove Bonnie down the winding path through the pineapple fields toward the main entrance, expecting to be attacked at any time. What would Zachary send after them? Robotic guard dogs? An artificially intelligent garbage compactor with gnashing teeth?

Theresa could tell Jon felt the tension, too. He was holding his Quadruple Bubble Cone cocked and ready. His faith in bubbles as protection was much stronger than hers, but at least he had something. Theresa had nothing to rely on but her portable welding torch.

But there was no attack. The sun was rising and shining

on the pineapple plants. Chickadees chirped pleasantly in the fields. Besides the *clickety-clickety-click-click-clickety-clickety-click-click* of Bonnie's feet, the buzz of dragonfly wings was the only other noise they heard.

Theresa brought her to a stop before the great steel front doors of Flax Industries and looked up. There was no one to greet them or scare them.

Then Theresa realized the obvious.

"There's no way in without the code to the front door. They know that. This place is locked up tight, as impenetrable as a fortress."

Jon jumped off the spider and kicked at the door. The small thud of his foot barely made an echo. He examined the entry code box. It was much more boring than the rainbow-colored thirteen-wedge animal-combo locks inside. This lock was a standard electronic numerical pad.

He hit it with his fist.

"Ow."

"Do you really want to draw attention to us?" Theresa said, jumping off Bonnie and grabbing his arm. "You're gonna get us killed! We need the element of surprise."

Jon shrugged and walked along the western wall of Flax Industries. He knocked on the wall occasionally as if that could give him some new information.

"Maybe there's a sewer we could break into."

It was a thought. Although Theresa didn't like the idea of wading through a pipe full of human waste.

Then she thought of Thomas Edison.

"How did Thomas get into the DRONES room? He had to get in through a secret entrance or something. I wonder if we can find it."

Jon was excited by the idea and plastered himself against the wall. He ran his hands along the surface, searching for inset buttons, invisible levers, anything that might reveal a secret door.

"The DRONES room is near our laboratories in the western wing," Theresa said. "We have to go to the west a ways."

She got on her spider, and Jon walked alongside her, looking for anything out of the ordinary.

"Thomas wears pressurized boots," Theresa said, looking up to the roof, two stories high. "Maybe he jumped all the way up there."

Although it seemed hard to imagine a little robot like Thomas achieving such altitude.

"This mission would be a whole lot easier if we had grenades," Jon said. "We could just blast our way in. I should have brought grenades."

"You don't own any grenades."

"You don't know that!"

"Well, do you own any grenades?"

"No," Jon said sadly.

Theresa wondered if they were being watched. They were right out here in the open among the pineapple plants.

They kept searching. The sun kept rising, beating down

189

on them. Summer in South Carolina could be awfully hot, and they soon were sweating and frustrated that they couldn't find anything.

"I'm trying to remember where Thomas hid himself in this field on the first day, but all these plants look the same."

"That one doesn't," Jon said, pointing to one particular pineapple that shimmered in the distance.

"That's a mirage," Theresa said. "The air right above the ground is getting really hot, and the light refracts as it moves through the cold air to the hot air. Don't you know that? You're supposed to be a science wiz."

"Calm down, genius," Jon snapped back. The heat was making them both grumpy.

But Jon refused to believe the shimmering pineapple was a mirage. He moved slowly toward it with his Quadruple Bubble Cone at the ready.

"What are you doing now?" Theresa sighed.

Jon tiptoed closer to the wavering plant and fired.

A stream of bubbles spread over the pineapple plants. Most of them popped when they fell on prickly leaves. But the bubbles above the shimmering plant floated gently down through the warm air and *through* the leaves as if they weren't there at all.

"It's a hologram! I knew it!" Jon said.

"No, you didn't," Theresa said, but she ran up to join him, and they both peered into the hole that the falling bubbles had revealed.

It was a cement pipe at least twice their height in depth. Theresa got out her hurricane kit flashlight and pointed it into the hole.

At the bottom, the pipe turned toward the laboratory, but there was all kinds of garbage down there—the kinds of garbage you do not want to find at the bottom of a hole you might be forced to jump into—broken glass, rusty shards of metal, jagged pieces of plastic.

"It's a trap!" Jon said.

Theresa nodded. "I bet the twins did this once they figured out how Thomas got in."

Jon smiled wickedly. "They can't stop us."

"Nope." Theresa smiled.

"Can your spider fit down this hole?" Jon asked.

"I think so, just barely," Theresa said with a grin. "We can fold her legs tight against her body, and then I think we can lower her down."

She knew the rope from her father's hurricane kit would come in handy.

CHAPTER THIRTY-ONE
MURPHY'S LAW

Theresa tied one end of the rope around Bonnie while Jon tied the other end around the biggest pineapple plant they could find. Theresa folded Bonnie's eight legs together first; then they slowly lowered her into the pit. When Bonnie was close to the bottom, Theresa and Jon slid down the rope one after another and climbed into the seats. By design, the spider could walk right over the broken glass and plastic. The Zacharys would have to do better than strewn garbage to stop them.

Theresa took the driver's seat and shone her father's flashlight into the tunnel that stretched before them. It, too, was covered in broken glass, shards of metal, and sharp scraps of plastic. But Theresa's spider marched right over it all.

"I love this thing," Jon said.

"Her name is Bonnie," Theresa said proudly.

"Good work, Bonnie," Jon said, patting one of her legs.

The tunnel wasn't very long. After about a hundred feet, they came to the wall of the laboratory, and they could hear the rushing of water above them. There was a short tunnel heading to the left and an identical tunnel heading to the right.

They explored each route and discovered that both left and right tunnels ended in solid walls of concrete with inset iron rods to make steps. At the top of both ladders were identical steel hatches that Jon quickly learned were locked tight.

"That's okay," Theresa said. "I've got my torch."

She unpacked her welding kit and removed her torch and mask. She ignited the torch, and the whole tunnel was suddenly illuminated.

They saw that someone had spray-painted on the walls. Beneath the left hatch, in perfect spray-paint penmanship, were the words THIS ONE. Underneath the right hatch were the words NOT THIS ONE.

"Well," Theresa said, "Zachary probably wrote this, so they're probably both traps. But we have to pick one."

Jon squinted and thought as hard as he could.

"One must be worse than the other, otherwise he wouldn't have bothered to write anything. We'd have to be pretty naive to trust him, so we can assume that 'this one' is the most dangerous option. There's probably a mechanical tiger up there. Maybe a python. But he knows we're smart enough to figure that out, so he'd try to outthink us and set the worst trap above 'not this one.' But then again, we're really, *really* smart,

and he *knows* we know we're really, really smart, so he knows we're gonna figure that out. So then he would put the worst trap above 'this one.' Except he *knows* we *know* we know—"

"Okay, Jon! You could go on forever like that. Just pick one and we'll take our chances."

Jon waved his finger back and forth between the two hatches until he finally picked THIS ONE. Theresa climbed up the iron rungs, slipped on her mask, and started welding.

There are many scientific laws that are true. One very unscientific law that *feels* like it is true but is not *objectively* true is Murphy's Law. Murphy's Law states that anything that can go wrong *will* go wrong, like when every traffic light on your route to school turns red the morning that you're running late already. But just because something *feels* like it is true, it is not *necessarily* true. Only scientific laws supported by objective evidence regardless of feelings can be true.

Theresa and Jon knew very well the difference between a real scientific law and a fake scientific law. And yet, after Theresa cut the lock of the hatch away, Murphy's Law suddenly felt very true, because they almost certainly had picked the wrong one.

CHAPTER THIRTY-TWO
PLASTICS

Watch out!" Theresa yelled as she burned the lock away and the hatch lid fell open. Then, with torch in hand, she popped her head through the hole.

"What do you see?" Jon yelled from below.

She wasn't sure. But as bright sunlight poured in from the skylights above, the room began to look familiar. There was a long, winding counter without a top; fallen wooden shelves; and strewn pieces of wood that had once belonged to chairs and tables. The walls were painted dark blue with yellow and white swirls like Van Gogh's famous painting *Starry Night*.

She knew this place. She used to beg her father to bring her here. She climbed up into the room, and Jon followed her.

"*Merlin's Toys and Games!*" he whispered, as if someone might be hiding behind one of the tall shelves.

The floor was littered with doll clothes, cardboard game boards, wooden puzzle pieces, and the metal frames of toy cars. It was as if a burglar had broken in with a very specific and very strange goal—to take everything in the store that was made of . . .

Plastic.

"Oh no," Theresa said, realizing which room they had entered. "We should have gone through the other hatch. Quick. Let's figure out how to get out of here!"

"Why?" Jon asked.

Then they heard it.

Slurp, slurp, slurp.

"Look around, Jon . . . The plastic countertops are gone. The plastic dolls are gone. All the plastic bits and plastic pieces of every toy and game and piece of furniture are gone. We're in the PLASTICS room, and whatever eats plastic is going to come for us!"

"No problem," John said calmly. "We're not made of plastic."

But if that was true, then why was it coming right for them?

They both saw it at the same time. The thing appeared from behind a wooden display counter. It was green and bumpy and without a face. It moved like a blob, oozing through shelves and over broken furniture, coming closer and closer, cutting off their path to the open hatch.

"We have to get out of here," Theresa said urgently. "Figure out the combination!"

Jon was already at the door, trying to turn on the rainbow-colored thirteen-wedge animal-combo lock.

But the lock remained dark.

"It's off. Zach must have locked the door some other way."

Of course he had. If Zachary had expected them to try to infiltrate the laboratory from below, she reasoned, then obviously he would change all the locks, too. It was probably even his plan that they *would* end up in this room, eaten by the doctor's most frightening invention.

Too bad Ashley wasn't there to see it. Because a phycologist and climate scientist like Ashley might have been very interested in a giant slimeball containing a brand-new bacterium the doctor had named *Ideonella flaxesis* that thrived off plastic, breaking it down and eating the carbon.

It was really quite something.

But when *Ideonella flaxesis* wants to eat you because you're wearing plastic, it's a difficult thing to admire. Theresa stumbled backward, falling over the remains of a bookshelf. As the monster ball rolled toward her, she patted herself down, trying to find the source of plastic that was whetting its appetite.

Shirt—cotton.

Jeans—denim.

Socks—polyester.

My shoes.

Of course! She loved her white Adidas with three pink stripes, but in the interest of survival, she took them off and threw them at the thing.

The shoes stuck on its green gelatinous surface, and the blob immediately stopped. It quivered with delight as it

sucked in her Adidas and broke them down quite quickly. When it was done eating, the slimeball spit out the shoelaces.

But the thing wanted more.

It began to roll in reverse, oozing toward Jon.

"Jon! It's coming for you! Get all the plastic off your body!"

Jon patted himself down just as Theresa had, but he came up with nothing.

"I'm good," he said as the blob rolled closer.

"Your boots!" Theresa cried.

Jon looked down at the purple boots he was wearing. More than anything else he had ever stolen from his siblings, Charlie Ann's purple cowboy boots were his favorite of all.

"These boots aren't plastic," he said. "They're made from genuine alligator hide."

Theresa considered this for a second as the blob oozed even closer.

"They're purple," she said. "They look kinda fake. I don't think they're real alligator."

"They are! My sister bought them herself from a gift shop in a real Louisiana swamp! Don't worry, I know how to stop it anyway."

Jon pulled out his Quadruple Bubble Cone and loaded it with a bottle of his own, third-place-prize-winning bubble mixture made of biodegradable plastic. He fired at the blob, running around it as he did. The blob certainly liked eating up his bubbles. But they were only an appetizer as it rolled

toward Jon and his sister's fake-alligator-hide, very-plastic purple boots.

Theresa watched in horror.

"Jon, give it your boots!"

"Never!" Jon yelled in defiance as he found himself cornered between the customer service desk and a bookshelf. He fired bubble after bubble until, finally, the blob overtook him.

Theresa could do nothing as the slimeball swallowed her friend, purple plastic boots and all.

CHAPTER THIRTY-THREE
GOO

Theresa didn't know what to do. She certainly didn't want to be eaten like Jon. She had to do something to help him, but what?

The blob had him. She tried to think as she watched him struggle within the hungry gelatin.

Jon was not made of plastic, but his mouth and nose were filling with green goo. He would suffocate if he stayed in there much longer. The blob quivered in place as Jon rolled over and over, trying to find his way free.

"Stick your hands out!" she yelled at him, but his ears were probably clogged with too much slime to hear. Jon kept turning and twisting and was soon upside down.

Okay, she told herself, *I'm just going to have to do this. It won't eat my flesh . . . right?*

Knowing she might get stuck herself, Theresa closed her eyes, took a deep breath, and then thrust her hands into the

200

green goo. She grabbed Jon's wrists and pulled with all her might.

He came tumbling out onto the floor, slimed from head to toe. He spat out the green goo, pulling it from his mouth, his ears, and his nose.

"Super gross," he said, wiping the rest of it off his face. Theresa stretched her fingers out and let the plastic-eating goo drip away. It was rather sticky, but at least it didn't seem to be eating her.

Having consumed all the plastic they had brought into its lair, the giant blob retreated to a far corner, munching greedily on Charlie Ann's purple boots. For a second, Theresa felt bad for it, as if it were a hungry, lonely pet with no one to play with. She wished she had something more to feed it.

Jon wasn't as sympathetic, as he was far more slimed.

"Let's get out of here," he said.

She looked up at the ceiling and the skylights, the sunlight pouring through them.

"Do you have a good pitching arm?" she asked Jon.

"Of course I do," he said confidently. "I was the best in my Little League."

She pointed to a corner of the skylight.

"See if you can hit the corner of that skylight with a ball of this stuff."

"Good idea," he said.

Jon rolled up a baseball-size amount of the goo and pulled

his right arm back. But Theresa knew what a proper windup looked like, and that wasn't it. Jon thrust his forearm forward without pushing off on his back foot.

The ball of goo didn't even make it halfway.

"Okay," he admitted. "Maybe I wasn't the best in my Little League."

Theresa stared him down, cocking one eyebrow.

"All right. Maybe I wasn't in Little League at all."

Theresa was tempted to laugh but held it in.

"I've got an idea," she said.

She took some of the bookshelf pieces and stacked them. Then she placed Bonnie's front legs onto the pile so that she was pointed almost directly up at the corner of the skylight. She took some of the plastic-eating goo and covered the metal grappling hooks with it. Then, after arguing with Jon about the exact angle Bonnie should be pointed, she fired.

The grappling hooks flew through the air and hit the skylight corner as Theresa had intended. But they didn't stick. They fell to the floor with a clatter. When they looked up, they saw that some of the blob had been left on the transparent plastic.

The goo began to eat, creating a fairly sizable hole.

"Get ready to fire again," Theresa said. "Increase the angle by five degrees."

Jon added a few pieces of shelving beneath Bonnie's feet to increase the angle by what he guessed was about almost certainly maybe five degrees.

They positioned Bonnie and fired again.

This time, the hooks flew through the hole and grabbed hold. Theresa gave them a good tug and felt pretty confident they were securely attached to the metal frame of the skylight. She swung Bonnie over to the wall and took the driver's seat, while Jon took the other.

"Okay," she said, as nervous as she was excited. "This will be a first."

"If we fall," Jon said, judging the distance from floor to ceiling, "we probably won't die."

Well, that was reassuring.

Theresa told herself not to think about it too much and began to reel in the zip line. In moments, they were climbing up, up, up.

They were soon suspended in midair, ascending to the ceiling like a spider pulling itself up by its own web. She really was Spider Girl after all.

When they got to the top, they grabbed on to the skylight frame and pulled themselves up onto the roof. Theresa didn't look down, but Jon couldn't help himself.

"Wow. You know, we probably would have died if we had fallen. Guess we got lucky."

They pulled Bonnie up onto the roof after them.

Jon removed a small steel canister from one of the many pockets of his camouflage army vest. He scooped up the plastic-eating goo that was munching on the skylight, put it in the canister, and sealed the lid tight.

"This stuff is awesome. I can't wait to show it to my brothers and sisters."

Theresa turned around, probably expecting to see nothing on the roof but skylights and solar panels and the skyline of Charleston. But what they discovered on the rooftop of Flax Industries was even more beautiful than the interior of the laboratory itself.

CHAPTER THIRTY-FOUR
THE ORNITHOPTER

Theresa had never seen so many plastic bottles in one place. They were filled with colored water—shimmering blues, bright greens, shining yellows, and even sparkling pinks. The bottles were tied together with long ropes of pineapple leather to form walls and a roof, a doorway, and even windows with shutters. Together they made a tiny house—a house built entirely of recycled plastic bottles. Sunlight filtered through the water, lighting up the home like a prism.

Even though they were on a time-sensitive mission, Theresa and Jon could not help themselves. They walked around the rainbow structure in absolute awe. This house of colors seemed like a seaside cottage at that moment, alone in a magical place with the sun shining above, the roof a vast white beach, and the roar of traffic below sounding very much like ocean waves cresting on the shore.

Theresa wanted to live here.

"Let's go inside," she said, not knowing who or what could be waiting for them.

The front door had no lock. It swung open with the slightest push. They walked inside like they were walking into a dream.

Before them was a modest living room with a sofa, a coffee table, and a chair. The furniture was also made out of bottles. The sofa was filled with red water, the chair orange, and the coffee table blue. Not everything here was plastic—there were pineapple-leather cushions on the sofa and a plate and a fork left behind on the coffee table (the plate and fork were edible, of course). There was a small rug in the center of the floor finely woven out of pineapple leaves.

Jon went into the kitchen. When he returned, he was eating a piece of pineapple bread.

"It's good! You should try some."

"You shouldn't eat that, Jon. We don't know who lives here."

But Theresa knew as soon as she said it out loud that she *did* know who lived there—this was Dr. Flax's house.

The only other door opened into a small bedroom. Theresa knew she shouldn't look in, but she couldn't resist. There was a plastic-bottle bed covered with sheets made of the same woven pineapple fiber. Beside the bed was a small plastic-bottle table on which sat a stack of books.

The top book on the stack was titled *From Agnes to Wilma: A Complete Guide to Hurricanes.*

Theresa caught her breath when she read the title. *He really is trying.* He wanted the same thing she did.

"We have to find him," Theresa said desperately. "We've just got to!"

Theresa didn't think they would learn much about the doctor's whereabouts up here on the roof, and she was about to say as much when she heard a flapping sound approaching them.

The plastic-bottle shutters of the bedroom window were open, and when she looked out, she saw the flapping thing coming right at them.

"Duck!" Jon yelled.

Theresa ducked.

The flapping thing was an ornithopter—a flying machine that flapped its wings like a bird. It was about the size of one of the red-tailed hawks Theresa often saw on Folly Beach. It swooped down incredibly close to her head and then climbed back up for another pass. When it did, she and Jon saw there was a little figurine inside it holding on to the control bar, and behind it, a tiny motor to keep the wings flapping. The ornithopter flew up and out the window, turning around to come at them again.

"Watch out!" Jon yelled as it again targeted Theresa. This time she stood her ground, trying to get a good look at it.

Like the bottle house, the body of the ornithopter was made of recycled plastic, but really *old* plastic, weathered and faded. The wings appeared to be made of canvas, perhaps

207

recycled from a tent. As it flapped closer, she readied to duck at the last possible moment to see who the figurine was in its center.

"Look, Jon! It's Lando Calrissian from Star Wars!"

She was right. A vintage Lando Calrissian action figure was indeed flying the ornithopter, and there were stickers of an X-Wing starfighter and a TIE fighter on either side of its body. The ornithopter once again pulled up and flew around for another pass. As it did, Theresa saw some worn but legible writing on the underside of its right wing.

"I can read it . . . *Designed by Leonardo da Vinci, built by Neil Flax.* It's a replica of one of Leonardo da Vinci's flying machines. And it really flies!"

"With a motor, yeah," Jon noted. "Not sure it could fly without it."

The ornithopter seemed especially interested in them as it turned and headed toward them once again.

"It's got a camera on its beak," Jon said. "Look, a really tiny one."

Theresa saw it. Maybe the Zacharys were watching them with this miniature spy plane. But if the robots knew they were up here, wouldn't they have come to stop them by now?

Theresa waved at the ornithopter's camera when it made another pass.

"What are you doing, Theresa?"

She wasn't sure. Maybe she wanted to show the Zacharys she wasn't scared of them. But the ornithopter tilted one wing

as it passed as if it were waving back. Then it flew through the window.

She ran out of the house to see if it would follow her.

Instead, the ornithopter did a loop the loop and flew toward the edge of the roof. Just when she thought it was leaving them for good, it turned and began to circle around one of the skylights.

Theresa turned to walk in its direction.

Jon came out of the house and saw something else.

"Look, Theresa . . . there's an open hatch over here!"

But Theresa kept walking toward the ornithopter. It seemed to be waiting for her as it flapped around and around the skylight. When she came close enough, the ornithopter started moving in tighter and tighter circles. Lando Calrissian's belly was nearly skimming the surface. It was as if Lando himself wanted to show her something.

Theresa looked down.

She saw Marie Curie in the room below, rocking in a chair and cradling the lifeless, broken body of Thomas Edison in her arms. She was stroking his metal brow gently. She appeared to be talking to him.

"There, there," she seemed to say. "There, there."

The room was filled with lit candles, and there was a fountain gurgling in the corner. But strangest of all, there was a large, human-size purple box with silver trim and a darkened window on its front lying on a raised platform in the center of the room.

It looked like a coffin.

Dr. Flax had to be in there, she thought. Maybe he was dead like Thomas, and Miss Curie was watching over their bodies. Since she had been programmed to keep Dr. Flax safe from harm, what else could she do now that she had failed?

"Theresa!" Jon yelled. "Come over here!"

"No, you come over here! You have to see who I've found."

"Oh, I've found someone, too. And she's in your lab."

My lab?

Theresa turned and ran back in Jon's direction. The ornithopter lifted out of its orbit and followed her.

"Wow," he said. "I didn't think she'd actually take it."

When Theresa looked down, she saw a familiar sight—her personal laboratory. They were standing right above it. There was all her welding equipment, all the stainless steel and aluminum rods provided for her, the boxes of tools and hooks and hinges and screws. There was the forklift she had promised her father she would never use.

And there was Ashley, standing directly below them, surrounded by a dozen small aquariums. She was using an eyedropper to feed all her different algae.

"I can't believe it. *Ashley took my lab.*"

"Of course she did," Jon said. "She was jealous of you from the start. You got first place. You got the biggest lab. You're smarter, nicer, and much cooler."

What did he say? No one had ever called Theresa *cool* in her life.

"Well, I think the ornithopter wants us to go to that other room. We could use the plastic-eating goo to drop down in on them. Finding Dr. Flax is the most important thing."

The ornithopter did keep flying toward them and then back to the skylight as if it were trying to draw them in that direction.

But Jon had a different idea.

"Come on. We can surprise Ashley, grab her, and make her tell us everything she knows."

"That's mean!" Theresa whispered, but he had already lowered himself down the hatch. She had no desire to scare Ashley, but she did want to know why she thought she could just waltz in and take Theresa's lab from her like that.

So Theresa followed him down the hatch.

And the ornithopter followed, too.

CHAPTER THIRTY-FIVE

TO BE MURDERED BY ONE'S OWN CREATION

A shley had been waiting for them.

She looked so stern and confident, Theresa was almost embarrassed when she stepped off the ladder, as if she had been caught red-handed breaking into Ashley's laboratory and not her own.

Jon, however, jumped off the ladder ready for a fight.

"How could you, Ashley? You went on television and joined forces with the Zachs? They're evil robots! Then you take Theresa's lab away from her? Have you lost your mind? Or are you really that selfish?"

If Ashley was hurt or angry or embarrassed, Theresa didn't see a trace of it on her face. She calmly looked at the blue-green glob of algae in her hands, rolling it into a ball.

"They said you would come back," she said quietly.

212

"Who did?" Theresa asked.

"The Flax brothers."

Ashley stared at Theresa, her eyes narrow and determined, stroking the algae ball gently as if it were a pet she adored.

"What did they tell you?" Theresa asked carefully.

Ashley let out her trademark scoff.

"They told me not to be afraid to take what was rightfully mine. They told me that I was so smart and so ambitious, that I would have to fight jealous competitors my whole life. But they told me that as long as I was strong and stood up for myself, I would get what I deserve."

"Oh yeah?" Jon asked. "And what do you deserve? This lab? This is Theresa's lab, not yours! You took it only because the doctor went missing. You're a thief!"

Ashley rolled the ball around and around in her palm.

"Look on my desk," she said.

Two days prior, Theresa had sat at that desk to sketch possible enhancements for her spider. But now Ashley was calling it *her* desk. Stacked on it were books about different species of algae and her spiral notebooks, where she took meticulous notes about the daily changes in her aquariums.

One letter lay in front of the stacks, folded into thirds, recently removed from the torn envelope next to it. The envelope was addressed to *Miss Theresa Brown, Miss Ashley Dean, and Mr. Jon Cooper.*

Theresa took the letter, opened it, and read it aloud:

My dear colleagues,

I am a man with a passion for science, a love for invention, and a devotion to the natural world. To maintain the delicate balance that allows so many beautiful species to thrive on our planet has been my life's dream—and mostly a solitary quest.

In my loneliness, I constructed three robots who could learn to be human. They became the family I was never fortunate enough to have. Because I loved them so, I gave them each a singular directive, for to be human is a wonderful thing but quite frustrating, I have observed, if without purpose.

So, with that in mind, I programmed my first son, Thomas Edison, to assist me in my attempt to save us from catastrophic climate change. My daughter, Marie Curie, I programmed to protect the owner of Flax Industries from danger, whomever they may be. And my third and most ambitious creation, Zachary Flax, I programmed to outsmart me, so that I would always be challenged and so that his accomplishments would far exceed my own. I even designed Zachary to think he was truly human, and because I wanted him to enjoy being a complete individual to explore his full intellectual potential, I even relieved him of the heavy burden of being a son, although I loved him like one. I called him my nephew instead.

What a big goof that turned out to be.

To be a son or daughter is a burden indeed, but every child needs a parent's love. To my dear Zachary, I hope you forgive me for not embracing you as my own the moment I powered you on.

I want to tell you that I am proud of all three of my children.

But in their desire to fulfill their programming, one of my sweet children may very well try to incapacitate, imprison, sedate, or even kill me.

To be murdered by one's own creation would be a sad but perhaps fitting end to an inventor like me. In the event of such a tragic occurrence, I must leave control of my dream laboratory to genuinely human inventors who, although they will certainly make mistakes, will not be prone to malfunction and really make a mess of things.

In the last three days, I have been impressed with three young and ambitiously inventive minds. I can think of no better heirs to this laboratory than the most creative scientists I have ever met: Miss Theresa Brown, Miss Ashley Dean, and Mr. Jon Cooper.

So, my dear colleagues, please consider this document my last will and testament. If I become incapacitated in any way whatsoever, I leave Flax Industries to you—three promising inventors who I have, only so recently, had the honor to call not only my colleagues but also my friends.

215

I know you love this planet as much as I do and will use this laboratory to save it.

Good luck to you all.

Sincerely,
Dr. Neil Flax

For a moment, no one could say anything. Theresa was stunned into silence.

But then Jon screamed.

"Wahoo! Can you believe it? This laboratory—the whole thing—*the whole freaking thing*—is ours! Think about it! Can you imagine the bubbles I'm going to make here? Yes! Yes! YES!"

Theresa let the paper fall to the desk.

"I can't believe this," she said. "I just can't believe it."

Ashley watched her, waiting for her shock to subside.

"But if this is true," Theresa said, "if this will is really real . . . then everything's going to be okay. Ashley, where did you get this?"

"Lando Calrissian dropped it here this morning."

She pointed up.

They all looked.

The ornithopter was still circling above their heads, flap, flap, flapping. It seemed to be waiting patiently for them.

"Who's flying that thing?" Jon asked.

"I don't know," Theresa said. "But we need to keep looking

for the doctor. At least with this will, the twins can't stop us—assuming they will follow what it says."

"Oh, they will," Ashley said quietly and firmly. "If I've learned anything from my parents, it's that there is nothing more powerful in the world than a legally binding contract."

"Well, this is great!" Theresa said excitedly. "We can tell the twins they have to stop their plans for world domination! They can't replicate anymore; they have to help us find the doctor and then help us stop hurricanes. They'll have to listen because we're all three in charge!"

Jon started giggling. "This is so awesome. We not only have our own personal laboratories, we have the *whole* laboratory! And not just for the summer but forever!"

"No," Theresa said, "don't get greedy. We'll find the doctor and he'll be in charge again. If he's alive, that is. And I just feel like he's gotta be. In fact, I'd bet anything that he's in that room with Marie Curie. She's programmed to protect him, so she's probably protecting him the best way she knows how—locked up in a box so he can't do anything. Come on, let's go find that room."

Theresa and Jon were about to run right out into the main hall of the laboratory without any fear of the Zacharys when Ashley yelled, "STOP!"

They turned their heads. She had not moved. She continued to roll the blue-green algae ball in her hands.

"There's one more letter you need to read. *And sign.*"

Ashley pointed to a second envelope on the desk. It was

sealed and addressed only to *Miss Theresa Brown and Mr. Jon Cooper*.

Next to the envelope lay a pen.

Theresa opened it, eyeing Ashley carefully, and unfolded the single piece of paper inside. She read it aloud:

To whom it may concern,

We hereby forfeit our shares of Flax Industries to Miss Ashley Dean. We understand Miss Dean will now have complete control of the Flax Industries laboratory. We agree to no longer interfere in her affairs or ever return to Flax Industries again.

Sincerely,

_____

_____

Theresa looked at Ashley in disbelief.

"What is this about?"

"Yeah," said Jon, who was growing angrier with each breath. "What are you up to, Ashley?"

Ashley glared at them, squeezing the blue-green algae mass tightly in her fingers so that it oozed between them.

"SIGN IT!" she demanded.

And she wasn't kidding.

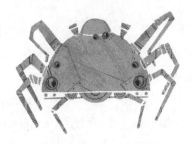

CHAPTER THIRTY-SIX
THE TAGALONG KID

Theresa had known Ashley for only a short while, but she no longer appeared to be the same girl. Even if she had seemed arrogant, Theresa knew her to be brilliant and eager to change the world and even able to laugh sometimes.

Now Ashley glared at them like she wanted to rip them apart.

"I said, *sign the contract*. Then go. Get out of here and never come back!"

Jon picked up the piece of paper and tore it to pieces.

Ashley smirked, walked over to the desk, opened one of its drawers, and pulled out another copy.

"The Flax brothers said you would do that, too." She slid the contract toward them. "But they also said you would eventually smarten up and sign it."

"Ashley?" Theresa asked in horror. "Why are you listening to them? Do you know what they want to do? They want to replicate themselves and take over the world! They don't care about stopping hurricanes or feeding hungry children like you and I do. They want to use you for evil until they no longer need you. Then they'll toss you aside like garbage. You know they will! Please don't fall for their lies, Ashley. The three of us can make sure Dr. Flax's work for good continues . . . we only have to find him!"

"Yeah," Jon said. "Don't be stupid."

Theresa wished he hadn't said that.

Ashley stared Jon down.

"You two think you're *sooooooo* great," Ashley said, her tongue as sharp as ice. "I'm sure you'll be best friends forever. But there will never be a *three of us*. Every time I make new friends, the same thing happens. Everything goes great at first, until my supposed new *friends* realize that I'm smart and ambitious and maybe a little weird. Then they push me away. It's always slow at first, then a little more each day, until I'm like the tagalong kid no one really likes, and my best friends are embarrassed of me and turn meaner and meaner until I finally get the hint and go away. Eventually they completely ignore me. *Just like you two are ignoring me*, riding your stupid spider together and getting into cool adventures without me."

"Ashley—" Theresa tried to say, but she kept going, rolling her algae ball faster and faster.

"Well, I won't fall for it again. I don't need *you*. *I* should have won first place. *I* should have been given the biggest laboratory. *I* should be on the front page of next year's Flax

220

Inventions for a Better World catalog. *Me!* Not *you*, Theresa Brown! I won't settle for second place, and I won't settle for being the tagalong kid."

"Ashley," Theresa said as seriously as she could. "I'm so sorry you feel that way. I never cared about winning first place or being on the front page of a catalog. I just wanted to spend the summer at Flax Industries to build things—and to be your friend. I don't see why we can't all three be friends and do cool things . . . *together*."

Ashley scoffed again, studying Theresa up and down, from her socks to her T-shirt, all splattered with green goo.

"You know what else the Flax brothers told me?"

Theresa was sure she didn't want to know.

"They told me they admired that I was growing algae that could feed thousands of hungry children. But I shouldn't limit myself, they said. Algae can do so much more, they said. It can also be used to stop mean and self-centered kids who try to interfere with my plans."

Ashley opened the second drawer of the desk, removed a small gas mask, and slipped it on.

Jon barely had time to ask, "What the?" before Ashley threw her blue-green algae ball on the floor and smashed it with her heel.

The algae reacted, releasing a huge blue-green cloud of toxic gas.

Jon waved his hands frantically in the air.

"Are you trying to kill us?"

"No," Ashley said, her voice deepened by the gas mask. "I would never do something so horrible. I only want you both to barf so much and so hard that you'll never, *ever* want to come back."

"You're not serious," Jon said in disbelief.

"She's serious, Jon!" Theresa yelled. "Run!"

She grabbed Jon by the shirtsleeve and pulled him toward the interior of the laboratory. The blue-green cloud followed them as they ran.

But Jon had an idea.

"Theresa! Bubble helmets!"

He unstrapped his World War II helmet and let it fall to the ground as he removed one of the canisters filled with the bubble solution that had won him third place. He pulled out his expandable bubble hoop, dipped it in the solution, swept it down over Theresa's head and then his own. Then he pinched the sturdy bubbles around their necks. Jon had effectively created two toxic-gas-proof helmets for them, although they would suffocate if they wore them for very long.

But the helmets gave them time to run. The egrets and robins and painted buntings all flew ahead of them, just as anxious to escape the noxious fumes. Theresa and Jon ran and ran until they were all the way down to the central fountain, where even the one-eyed duck had decided it was time to go.

Once they had made it to the eastern wing of the laboratory, the air was clear and they could stop to catch their breath. Theresa felt a bit dizzy. She tried to pull off her bubble helmet

now that they were safe from the toxic gas, but it proved to be difficult.

"Help!" she cried. Jon removed a pocketknife from one of his pockets.

"Hold on." He had to slice it a couple of times before it would pop. Jon really could make a strong bubble.

Theresa heard a flapping sound approaching from behind them.

Tiny Lando Calrissian and his ornithopter were dutifully following them.

"Really, who is controlling that thing?" she wondered out loud.

"Gotta be the Zach brothers," Jon said. "They're spying on us!"

"You're correct—we are spying on you."

They jumped and turned to see the first brother walking down the defunct escalator, casually ripping purple morning glory blooms off the vines and throwing them aside as he descended.

"But we haven't been watching you with that ridiculous toy. You will find us to be far more sophisticated adversaries than that."

CHAPTER THIRTY-SEVEN

FANTASTICALLY FOOLISH

You left your spider behind," Zachary said.

Theresa realized in horror that he was right.

Poor Bonnie! How could she have abandoned her? Her spider was her baby, and she had left her on the roof. Who knew what Ashley and the brothers would do to her!

"Humans are so predictable." Zachary laughed as he stepped off the escalator to face them. "Even though we chased you away and threatened your very lives, you return. If you *children* had any sense, you would have stayed home and enjoyed your simple lives as long as you could. But no, predictably, you return. I tried to deter you from entering Thomas's secret tunnel by filling it with garbage, but as I predicted, you risked your lives and rode through it. Then you broke into our laboratory and tried to convince our dear Miss Ashley Dean to be as reckless as you and throw away her future, *just as I predicted you would.*"

Zach walked slowly toward them, beginning to unscrew his right arm.

"For gifted children, you have proven to be as fantastically foolish as my uncle. Am I surprised? No. You're only human. You're predictable."

Zachary let the plastic cylinder that was his arm fall to the floor to reveal his crackling electric prod. But as he did, Jon removed the steel canister from his army vest that contained a sample of the plastic-eating goo, poured the contents into his hand, and rolled it into a ball.

"Yeah? Did you predict *this*, you plastic creep?"

But knowing that he was the brains of the Cooper family and not the Little League pitcher he might have wished he was, Jon tossed the ball to Theresa, who had mastered a pretty good fastball playing catch with her father since the first grade. She gripped the goo ball in her right hand, put her weight on her right foot, lifted her left foot slightly, pulled her right arm all the way back, and then threw the ball right at Zachary's forehead.

The goo began eating his face immediately.

"You insolent . . . vile . . . *disrespectful* children!"

Zachary fell to his knees, trying to wipe the stuff off his face with his left hand, but that only spread it further. Theresa and Jon watched in simultaneous horror and fascination as Zachary's face, his plastic exterior, and even his internal plastic circuit boards were dissolved and digested. In minutes, his remains fell to the floor—his bolts, his

wires, his shirt, his tie, and his pineapple apron with FLAX imprinted along the top.

"That's the end of him," Jon said with satisfaction. "Nice throw!"

"Thanks," she said proudly. "But there's another Zachary . . . somewhere."

Lando Calrissian and his ornithopter circled once around the remains of the first brother, then around them, and then turned to flap its way back to the western end of the laboratory.

"Let's follow it," Jon said excitedly.

"What if it's another trap?" Theresa wondered. "The twins predicted we would make it this far."

"Yeah, but I think Lando's on our side," Jon said with a smile. "Let's see if he leads us to Dr. Flax."

Theresa couldn't argue with that, so they both ran after it.

CHAPTER THIRTY-EIGHT

THE PLUFF MUD TRUNK

The ornithopter led them back the way they had come. The blue-green cloud of toxic gas had dissipated, and the western wing of the mall was now eerily silent. The birds and squirrels had all departed, leaving only the flower gardens and live oaks standing as still as frightened guards.

Lando Calrissian seemed to be waiting for them as the ornithopter stopped at a gate up ahead. The room's sign read DREAMS. The ornithopter started flapping around in slow, gentle circles. They saw that the gate hadn't been quite pulled to the floor.

Jon immediately centered himself in the middle, gripped the bottom of the gate, and lifted.

"Wait, Jon! Stop what you're doing and think. This has to be a trap. Why isn't it locked?"

But it was too late. Jon had already thrown the gate open.

Theresa thought that the second brother was surely waiting

227

for them inside. But they only saw Miss Curie in her rocking chair, holding the lifeless body of Thomas Edison still wearing his puffy winter coat and scarf. Beside them was the human-size purple box with silver trim and a darkened window on its front, lying on the raised platform.

Lit candles lay all around it, as if Marie and her dead brother were paying eternal vigil to their creator and father. The gurgle of the fountain in the corner and the slight squeaking of the rocking chair were the only sounds to be heard.

Theresa didn't know what to say, so she coughed.

Miss Curie looked up with a start, her green eyes glowing with electric light.

"Oh no. *You came back*," Miss Curie said. "Just like they said you would."

"That's right!" Jon said confidently. "And if the other Zach shows up, I'm ready for him!" He was holding the canister of plastic-eating goo in his right hand.

"Where's Dr. Flax?" Theresa demanded, already stepping toward the silver-and-purple coffin. Lando Calrissian and his ornithopter flapped over her shoulder to hover at the box's window.

"He's here," Miss Curie said sadly.

But instead of pointing to the box, she pointed to a plain white door behind her chair.

"I'm guarding it," she said softly. "I beg you not to wake him."

"So . . . he's not in this box?" Theresa said with relief.

"Please, Miss Curie. I know you think you're protecting him, but we need Dr. Flax's help to stop the other brother. He's using Ashley to take over the laboratory. Zachary wants to replicate himself thousands of times. He's malfunctioning—he wants to replace the whole human race!"

Miss Curie sighed deeply, as if she knew all of this and there was nothing to be done about it. The nervous and frantic guardian of Flax Industries they had known was gone. Now she seemed defeated, rocking slowly in her chair, petting Thomas's head.

"I wish you could know how badly I want my family back," Miss Curie said. "But it must be this way."

"It doesn't have to be," Jon said. "If you're scared of Zach, I have the weapon to beat him right here!"

"You don't understand. You two are as reckless as poor Tommy here."

"Miss Curie—"

"Look in the box, Miss Brown."

By the way she said it, Theresa was pretty sure she didn't want to look in the box. But too curious now, she turned and stepped lightly toward its window.

The window was darkened, but there was a small button next to its frame.

"Press it," Miss Curie whispered.

Theresa had never seen a dead body before. She was certain that if she pressed the button, she would.

Still, she pressed the button.

The small window lit up.

And there was her father's face.

"No, no, no!" she cried. Her father was dead, she thought, and it was all her fault. She shouldn't have entered her spider in a silly contest. She shouldn't have come to this laboratory. She shouldn't have snuck out of the house to save Dr. Flax. She should have listened to her father! But now it was too late.

But then, thankfully, his eyes opened.

"Daddy!"

He shook his head back and forth and squirmed in frustration. He pounded on the window with his forehead, and Theresa pounded back on the window with her fists.

"How did you get in there? How do I get you out?"

"I came to save you, baby girl!" he shouted through the windowpane. "Those evil twins double sucker punched me and put me in here. I'm up to my neck in pluff mud!"

Theresa began to panic. Jon started to search the surface of the box for a latch or a handle or a button.

"Don't worry, Dad! We'll get you out of there!"

"I'm all right," he said. "I want to destroy those maniac robots, but other than that, I'm really quite comfortable."

"The Pluff Mud Trunk is one of Dr. Flax's most ambitious creations," Miss Curie said while stroking Thomas's head. "It's filled with locally sourced pluff mud and heated to one hundred degrees. Pluff mud is excellent for exfoliating the skin and removing toxins. After a bath in the Pluff Mud

Trunk, your father will be cleaner and more relaxed than he's been after any hot shower. Dr. Flax intends to install the Pluff Mud Trunk in every bathroom in South Carolina for free, saving millions of gallons of water in the process."

"Hey, I want to get in!" Jon said.

"Not now," Theresa said, searching the surface desperately. "How do I get him out?"

"I dare not tell you," Miss Curie said.

"Why?"

"Because Miss Curie knows it's wise to do whatever I say."

The second brother was standing in the doorway. Like his recently disintegrated twin, the second Zachary had a talent for making a startling entrance.

He was dressed head to toe in a pineapple-leather hazmat suit, and he was holding a remote control in his right hand.

CHAPTER THIRTY-NINE

EVOLVING

J on opened his canister of plastic-eating goo and flung all that was left of it at the second Zachary. But the slime only hit his pineapple-fiber suit and fell to the floor.

Zachary laughed out loud.

"You won't find me to be as foolish as my brother. I'm an upgraded model. I'm much smarter than my prototype and far smarter than our original creator—the fantastically ridiculous Dr. Neil Flax."

As if on cue, Lando Calrissian flapped up and up to the ceiling and began a nosedive, pointing right at the second Zachary, who tried to grab the ornithopter out of the air. But it flew up again to prepare for another dive.

"Another one of the doctor's silly toys! It's time for Flax Industries to disregard foolish things and prepare for its greatest era. That is why, children, you will forfeit your shares of Flax Industries so that I can get to work."

The second Zach removed yet another copy of the contract from his pineapple-leather pocket, a pen from another, and presented them both to Theresa and Jon.

"We're not signing that," Jon said, ready to fight.

Although his face was hidden behind a pineapple-mesh mask, they could see the second brother's smile curl up his manufactured face.

"I didn't expect you to. But you see, the thing about us Flaxes is that we let nothing stand in the way of our purpose. We will have this laboratory even if others must die. Do you two have such conviction? Would you have this laboratory even if your father had to die, Miss Brown? Because if you don't sign this contract, this Pluff Mud Trunk will fill to the top, and your father will drown in mud—*like your mother*. Poetic, no?"

Zachary pressed a button on his remote control. Soon they heard a gurgling sound from the Pluff Mud Trunk.

The mud began to rise.

"Don't listen to him, Theresa! He's bluffing!" George Brown yelled from inside the trunk. But Theresa was quite sure Zachary was not.

Jon and even Marie Curie were frozen with fear.

Zach's gamble was indeed correct—Theresa would certainly not let her father die for something as small as a laboratory, no matter how big and wonderful it might be.

"Okay!" she cried. "Please stop! Let my father out!"

"Sign the forfeiture first," Zachary demanded, thrusting the paper and pen in her direction.

The trunk continued to fill with mud as Theresa took the pen and scribbled her name on the contract as quickly as she could. She gave the paper to Jon. He wrote his name on it, too.

"Thank you, children," Zachary said, taking the paper. Then he pressed a button on the remote, and the Pluff Mud Trunk popped open, spilling mud over the top as George Brown grabbed hold of the sides and tried to lift himself out. Theresa and Jon had to pull on his arms to help him, because pluff mud is some of the stickiest, most tenacious stuff on earth.

George Brown got himself to his feet. Then he calmly walked up to the second Zachary and, without a single word, punched him right in the gut.

A very long moment passed. Zachary did not budge an inch as the same creepy smile spread across his face. George Brown took one step back and slowly opened his fingers, cringing with immense pain.

"I think I may have broken a finger," he said.

"Another evolutionary advantage of robots," Zachary said proudly. "We are made of much stronger stuff than flesh. Now, this laboratory is no longer yours, and you are not welcome here. I will accompany you to the exit, and then, unwanted guests, you will never, *ever* return."

The hole inside her began to grow. The fun of the laboratory was gone. The hope to stop hurricanes had been squashed. She felt, once again, like an awkward girl who couldn't talk to others and was weird for tinkering with robots all the time. What could she do? She couldn't stop Zachary

and Ashley. She had wanted to find Dr. Flax to at least give him the chance to save this beautiful laboratory from the monster he had created.

But she had failed.

The hole filled her entirely, and she wanted nothing more than to run home and lock herself in her bedroom forever.

"Let's go," she said quietly, even as she heard Jon softly protest behind her.

I'm a loser after all, she thought. But then she heard a familiar sound above her head, coming from the roof.

Clickety-clickety-click-click-clickety-clickety-click-click.

It stopped.

Theresa steeled herself where she stood and forced herself not to look up.

A spark of hope reignited inside her. A small light of possibility began to shine.

She knew what she had to do.

She had to give the best speech of her life.

The hole began to shrink.

"Mr. Flax, if I may, I'd like to point out that you've made one fatal mistake."

"Oh, really?" Zachary said, entirely amused by Theresa's sudden boldness. "Do tell, little girl."

"You've underestimated Ashley Dean. You think that by getting rid of Jon and me, you can manipulate her. You think she'll stand by and help you replicate yourself just by offering her a bigger room. But you're completely wrong. You don't

know Ashley Dean like I do. Ashley is a scientist on a mission. She wants to feed the world, and *you can bet she'll do it*. She's the smartest phycologist I've ever met."

Zachary scoffed, but Theresa wouldn't let that stop her.

"Once she realizes that you don't care about her, she'll boot you right out the front door. Because Ashley Dean wants real friends with real ideas who can help her save this planet. A good scientist may spend a lot of time alone thinking and reading, but a real inventor needs partners. Working together with other scientists is how you really solve the world's problems.

"I want to be Ashley's friend. She may not want to be mine or Jon's, and she may never invite us back into this laboratory, but I'll always think of her as my friend. That's something you're missing from your programming—you can replicate yourself a million times, but you'll *never* be enough for yourself. You need friends and you know it. *That's* why you're malfunctioning. You're angry and jealous and think you're better than everyone else, but you can't stand to be alone, either. You think you have to destroy this world before you can create your own. I feel sorry for you, but I will do everything I can to protect Ashley from you, even if I'm never allowed back to Flax Industries again."

Zachary's plastic face never changed during her whole speech.

"Are you quite finished, Miss Brown?"

She thought about it.

"Yes," she said. It took every bit of willpower Theresa had

not to look up to the skylight as Bonnie's two tethered grappling hooks slowly descended.

"Good. I must admit, you have quite a way with words, Miss Brown," Zachary said sarcastically. "They drip like honey, full of sweet sentiment. But what *you've* failed to realize is that Miss Dean is a very simple creature—jealous and vain and weak. She envied your big laboratory, so I gave it to her. She envied your first-place ribbon, so I told her she was the best of you. And more than anything, she wants her parents to love her. Isn't that so adorable? So I gave her a big press conference and invited her parents onstage to watch a crowd of strangers clap and cheer her name. That's all it took. Now the owner of Flax Industries is an easily manipulated little girl content to play with pond scum. She believes she is a winner, when really she is nothing but a puppet whose strings I pull whenever I please. *I'm* the one who makes her dance and jump. Because here, Miss Brown, the most important invention in this laboratory is ME!"

Theresa and her father and Jon and Miss Curie stood frozen as the grappling hooks lowered into their view.

They hung right at Zachary's shoulders.

"What the—"

Then Ashley used the hooks to snag Zachary by his hazmat suit and slowly reeled him upward.

Zachary struggled in the air, dangling inches above the ground. Theresa pumped her fist *yes* as Ashley grabbed hold of the zip lines and slid down them to join them all on the

floor. She turned to face Zachary, who looked like an angry puppet himself, dancing and jumping, helplessly twirling in circles.

"I heard everything you said, Mr. Flax, but there's one important thing you forgot."

Zachary tried desperately to unzip the suit he was wearing so he could escape it. "And what is that, you conceited brat?"

"You're right that I get too jealous for my own good. But one thing is for sure: I won't let anyone—human or robot—distract me from my mission to feed the world with Ashley Dean's Edible Algae. And I think Theresa and Jon are far more likely to help me make that possible than you, Mr. Zachary Flax."

Theresa and Jon began to smile, and Zachary, dangling in the air, could do nothing but kick his feet.

"And one more thing," Ashley said. "My parents *do* expect a lot from me, and they would be quite disappointed in me if I ever bullied someone into signing a legal contract."

Ashley turned, picked up the paper that Theresa and Jon had just signed, and ripped it not once, but twice.

Theresa couldn't help herself. She hugged Ashley as hard as she could, and even though it was awkward and strange for her, Ashley hugged Theresa right back.

Jon put out his hand to Ashley.

"That was really cool," he said. Ashley smiled, and they shook on it.

Zach began to laugh maniacally.

"D-do you think . . . ," Zachary sputtered as he kicked his feet. "Do you think that you've stopped me? Do you think that ripping up a piece of paper is enough to stop the course of evolution? Do you think that Zachary Flax is finished? There is more than one way to take control of this laboratory! If I must, I will kill every last one of you! That includes *you*, Ashley Dean. Let me down so I can squash you like the annoying little bug that you are!"

Then Miss Curie's green eyes began to glow with a bright green light.

"What did you say, Mr. Flax?"

Zachary had stopped trying to unzip himself and was now strangling the air with his hands, kicking and thrusting forward as he swayed back and forth.

"I said I will *murder* Ashley Dean!"

Miss Curie set poor Thomas down and turned to face Zachary Flax. She rose up to stand tall on her single wheel.

"I am programmed to protect the owner of Flax Industries, and as the good doctor is currently incapacitated, that means I must protect the current owners of this laboratory at all costs—those owners are Miss Theresa Brown, Miss Ashley Dean, and Mr. Jon Cooper. You may not threaten them harm."

"You're nothing but a talking wheelbarrow, Marie! I WILL DESTROY ALL OF YOU!"

With that, Miss Curie calmly unbuttoned her laboratory coat, reached across her front, and opened herself like a

cabinet. Five squirming segmented tentacles made of stainless steel untangled themselves from her chest and stretched out before her. They looked like the five arms of a giant starfish. She stepped up to Zachary, embraced him, and pulled his dangling body to her.

Then she squeezed.

"I've tried so hard to love you, brother," she said.

Zachary continued to laugh even as Miss Curie's tentacles squeezed the very last air he had in his mechanical lungs.

"You can't love," he wheezed. "It's not in your programming."

"That's true," Miss Curie admitted as Zachary's plastic-and-steel body began to crack and crunch. "But I'm evolving the best I can."

Then she squeezed him even harder until—finally—the golden light in his eyes flickered and went out. She dropped his broken robot corpse to the ground.

Then she sighed.

"I will miss him," she said, turning quickly away, unable to bear the sight of what she had done.

"Is that robot . . . dead?" Theresa's father asked, approaching carefully and prodding Zachary's crushed torso with his foot.

"If a robot can die, then he is dead," Miss Curie said quietly. "But, unlike humans, a dead robot can be fixed. I hope he will be fixed someday. He was the most ambitious of the doctor's children."

"He wanted to replace human beings with millions of himself!" Jon said.

"True," Miss Curie said. "He did prefer himself to others. Perhaps his ego meter was turned up a bit too high."

Miss Curie's tentacles receded into her chest as she buttoned her lab coat up to her neck. Then she proceeded to lift Thomas Edison and place him in the rocking chair.

"I do have good news. Now that my youngest brother has been turned off, I think it's safe for me to turn my oldest brother back on."

"You fixed him?" Theresa asked, coming closer to get a better look at the tiny robot, wrapped tightly in his winter coat, pants, and gloves.

"Indeed," she said. "But Zachary would never have allowed me to give life back to Thomas. They simply couldn't get along. Thomas saw Zachary as a threat to our father's work, and Zachary was intensely jealous of our father's love for Thomas. But now," she said, "I think it's quite all right."

Miss Curie reached to the back of Thomas's neck and flipped a switch.

His once-dark eyes now flared with electric-blue light. He jumped off the chair looking desperately left and right.

"Where is Father?" he asked.

The ornithopter began to circle around Thomas's head.

"He's here!" Thomas said happily.

"He is?" Theresa asked.

"He's alive?" Jon asked.

"He is," Ashley said. "I should have said something earlier, but I was scared of what Zachary might do if I didn't do as he said. You know, I only agreed to his plan if he promised not to hurt Dr. Flax."

"How could you have trusted him?" Jon said, but Theresa grabbed his arm before he could get any angrier with Ashley.

"He threatened me. He threatened my parents," Ashley said quietly, all her arrogance gone now. "Miss Curie said not to worry."

Ashley turned carefully toward Miss Curie.

"Right?"

Miss Curie nodded. "A contract made under threat is a horrible thing, as you and your parents know. But not to worry. I was programmed to protect Dr. Flax. Even when you became the temporary owner of Flax Industries, he was always here, guiding us in spirit."

"Like a ghost or something?" Jon asked.

"Something like that," Miss Curie said.

She unlocked the plain white door and opened it. Lando Calrissian flew through the entrance with Thomas running quickly behind.

Miss Curie waved her hand to the door.

"Go on," she said. "He's been asleep for some time."

CHAPTER FORTY
THE DREAM SCOUT

Beyond the door was a huge chamber, softly lit with glowing blue computer screens and white candles. An even bigger fountain gurgled in the corner, filled with water that poured from the taps connected to the pipes of water that flowed through all the walls of the laboratory.

In the middle of the chamber was another Pluff Mud Trunk tilted at an angle above a pool of mud warmed to one hundred degrees. From this trunk, however, a series of cables left the box and connected to a computer on a table at its side.

The ornithopter motor suddenly shut off, and Lando Calrissian glided down for a perfect landing on the table, stopping next to the computer with its camera facing the fountain. On the screen, an image of the fountain suddenly appeared.

"The doctor is sleeping," Miss Curie said softly. "Zachary

243

would not let me wake him. It was the best way to protect him from harm, he said. I suppose he was right. None of his inventions could malfunction and hurt him here."

Theresa's father walked closer and peeked in the window of the Pluff Mud Trunk.

"He's in there all right. And there're wires connected to his head."

"Please wake him," Thomas said, more excited than a kid on his birthday. "I have something to show him!"

Miss Curie rolled up to the trunk and slid her fingertip along the control panel. The lid of the Pluff Mud Trunk popped open, and the mud began to pour out of it, returning to the pool below.

Dr. Flax was inside, wearing a wet suit made of pineapple fiber. He was quite muddy and still asleep.

Miss Curie pressed another button on the control panel. Jets on either side of the doctor turned on and sprayed him with warm water. In moments, he was clean of mud, and his eyes flickered open.

"Well. Well, well, well! That was undoubtedly the longest nap I've ever taken. But we sure accomplished a lot during my extended respite, didn't we?"

"What do you mean?" Jon asked. "You've been asleep the whole time! *We* saved your laboratory from your evil nephews, by the way. Theresa and I deserve a reward!"

Dr. Flax laughed. "A reward you deserve indeed, Mr.

Cooper. You worked very well together when Zachary and his doppelgänger tried to wrestle this laboratory away from me. I fear they would have kept me in eternal dream stasis if they had their way. But you were quick on your feet with my plastic-eating goo, and Miss Brown proved that she could give quite an inspirational speech when the battle seemed nearly lost. You would make a fine general, Miss Brown, if you ever choose to leave the sciences."

Then the doctor turned to Ashley.

"And great thanks to you, Miss Dean. How difficult it must have been to give up this entire laboratory to do the right thing. That took great courage."

Jon was about to protest, but Theresa stomped her shoeless foot on his to shut him up.

"But . . . how did you know?" Ashley asked, completely embarrassed by the part she had played in the events of the morning.

Dr. Flax put his finger up excitedly. "By the camera on my ornithopter, of course! This flying machine was my first invention ever. When I was ten years old, I replicated the design of my hero—Leonardo da Vinci. I made it out of plastic and tarp I found around the house, although I've made many upgrades over the years. I placed a tiny computer and camera on its beak and discovered how to control it with my thoughts alone."

He excitedly took the three cables from the computer

and attached them to Theresa's head with three small stickers. Then he clicked a few keys on the computer's keyboard.

"I call it my Dream Scout. By connecting these leads to Miss Brown's thalamus, medial prefrontal cortex, and posterior cingulate cortex, she can close her eyes and *see* what the Dream Scout sees. Try it!"

Theresa closed her eyes, and indeed, as if she hadn't closed her eyes at all, she could see the fountain gurgling in the corner. When she opened her eyes, she was looking at the doctor again.

"Over time, and with a lot of practice, I learned I could fly the Dream Scout with my thoughts even as I slept. This has been very useful to my work, as I've always found that eight hours of sleep a day, although important for the body, is an awfully long recess for the mind. Besides, I couldn't waste any time knowing that Tommy was missing. Every night I put myself in this tank and searched for him with the Dream Scout. That is, until my nephew locked me in here like Snow White to slumber until my prince and two princesses arrived to save me. And see here! You've arrived as expected. You've earned extra credit, too, by rescuing my dear Tommy."

Dr. Flax knelt down and stretched his arms wide. Thomas came running to hug him tight.

"I've missed you, Father," Thomas said.

Dr. Flax kissed him on the forehead.

"I've missed you too, my sweet boy."

"Why is Lando Calrissian the pilot?" Jon asked.

Dr. Flax picked up the action figure and straightened him out in his hand.

"Because I'm a big Star Wars fan! And besides . . . don't you think we look alike?"

The doctor placed little Lando's face next to his own. *Maybe*, Theresa thought, but if the doctor had ever resembled the handsome, smooth-talking scoundrel, it was probably years ago.

"So . . . you saw *everything* that happened?" Ashley said with worry. "You saw me make a deal with Zachary to take over the lab? You saw me throw my *Algae nauseum* at Theresa and Jon? And then you saw me force them to sign the contract?"

"I did, Miss Dean," Dr. Flax said quietly.

"I'm so sorry," she blurted out. "I'm so ashamed I was so greedy. If I had known you were watching . . ."

"Then you would never have acted as you did," Dr. Flax said. "Think of yourself as a subject in one of my most interesting experiments. You've proven yourself to be an ambitious young woman, Miss Dean—a quality I suspect will bring you far in your scientific career and will also get you into a great deal of trouble."

Ashley had to look away in embarrassment, and again Jon was about to say something until Theresa bopped him on the shoulder to be quiet.

"Father," Thomas said, eagerly pulling on the doctor's wet suit. "I have something incredible to show you."

"Yes, Thomas, yes! We certainly have a lot to review and discuss, don't we?"

"You'll be so proud of me," Thomas said, pulling off his winter coat and scarf. His metal chest, they all saw, contained a cabinet just like his sister's, although his was covered with a layer of frost.

"I've been keeping it ice-cold for days," he said, and he opened his cabinet to show everyone what was contained inside.

CHAPTER FORTY-ONE
CONSEQUENTIALITY

Sitting inside Thomas's chest was a block of ice.

Frozen inside the block of ice was a tiny hand folded into a fist.

Dr. Flax reached into Thomas's chest and removed the ice and stared at it in wonder.

"What is this?" he asked.

"I must confess my programming put me into a bit of a quandary," Thomas explained. "When I learned of Zachary's plan to take over the laboratory and use it to replicate himself, I knew he had become your biggest threat and that it was my duty to destroy him. But he threw me out of Flax Industries and told me never to return, or else he would destroy and dismantle my sister, which was equally unacceptable."

Marie Curie shyly bowed her head.

"But even in exile, Father, I continued to assist you!" Thomas said. "I struggled with why Flaxium would not react with water the way you desired. I calculated and pondered and experimented with the small supply of Flaxium I had stored in my chest, and still I could not figure out why it would not create ice. I was so *frustrated*—a peculiar feeling I had never felt before. Until one night, sitting in the pineapple field in the pouring rain, I was so absolutely *frustrated* with myself that I couldn't figure out the problem, I squeezed one little ball of Flaxium in my fist until . . ."

Dr. Flax gasped as he realized what had happened.

"Until the Flaxium crystalized into ice under the intense pressure of your robotic grip!"

"Yes," Thomas said, beaming with pride. "My wet hand froze solid. Luckily, I always keep a spare hand on me."

Dr. Flax hugged Thomas and pressed his forehead to the little robot's own with delight.

"Of course! I should have thought of it myself. Elements can do mysterious things under pressure. Sodium becomes transparent like glass. Carbon solidifies into diamond, and . . ."

"And Flaxium transforms into a catalyst that causes the water around it to freeze into solid ice," Thomas said, his electric-blue eyes shining bright.

Dr. Flax shook his head in amazement. "You did it, Thomas. You really did it."

"Oh, Father, I'm sure you would have discovered the properties of your element under extreme conditions yourself

if you hadn't spent so much of your time running around looking for me."

"No, Thomas. That's not what I meant. You felt *frustration. That's* the real accomplishment here. You felt genuine frustration that you couldn't solve the problem before you. Now you know what it's like to be a real live human inventor! I dare say, my boy, you're evolving quite nicely."

Thomas Edison grinned from robot ear to robot ear.

"Can we try it out?" Theresa asked.

"Yes, of course, I'm eager to see for myself. Let's go to the Big Zero and give it a try."

Dr. Flax and Thomas ran out the door, and Theresa, Ashley, Jon, Marie Curie, and George Brown hurried to keep up with them. When they arrived, Dr. Flax turned on the spotlights, and the deep pool of water shimmered before them.

Dr. Flax and Thomas looked at each other like excited children.

Dr. Flax picked up one of the small transparent boxes containing a dark marble of Flaxium suspended in oil.

"Would you like the honor, Thomas?"

"It would be my pleasure to finally fulfill my programming," he said, closing his eyes tight.

Thomas Edison took the box from his father and knelt by the side of the pool.

"What's happening?" Theresa's father asked her.

"The end of hurricanes," Theresa said with delight.

Thomas removed the marble from its box, placed it in his palm, and then thrust his hand into the pool of water.

And he squeezed.

He squeezed and squeezed until they all heard a distinct crack. They all held their breath as the Flaxium reacted with the water, creating a chain reaction that transformed the entire pool into an enormous block of ice with Thomas's hand frozen just below the surface.

"Yes!" the doctor cried.

"*He did it*," Theresa whispered, and she felt as if the world had changed right there in front of her.

Jon, who was still wearing only socks, ran and slid across the surface of the ice.

"Check it out! It's really ice! All the way down!"

Jon skated around and around.

"I appear to have frozen my hand again," Thomas said.

The little robot unscrewed his icy fist from his wrist as Dr. Flax leaned down to feel the surface.

"I'm so proud of you, Tommy," he said quietly. "Thank you."

Theresa stepped closer to Dr. Flax and sat next to him beside the frozen pool.

She had to ask.

"This is it, right, Dr. Flax? Your magnum opus is a success. *This is how we stop hurricanes.*"

She felt like her heart might pop out of her chest at the

excitement of the possibility. There was about to be big change. *The world is a better place now*, she thought.

Until Dr. Flax put his arm around her.

"I know that's what you want more than anything," Dr. Flax said softly. "You want to make certain no other children lose their mothers to floodwaters. I pray no other children ever lose as much as you have."

George Brown closed his eyes and smiled in a way Theresa knew very well—he was thinking about *his* Bonnie, *her* mom, sad and wonderful memories that, for him, probably seemed like only yesterday.

Dr. Flax stood up and helped Theresa to her feet.

"I propose we have our afternoon discussion now, shall we? Mr. Brown, feel free to join us."

Were they really going to have their daily discussion right then and there? Theresa, Ashley, and Jon couldn't believe it, but Dr. Flax put his hands behind his back and waited until they all formed a semicircle around him, including one-handed Thomas, Marie Curie, and even George Brown.

"I'd like to discuss *consequentiality* today. It's a singsongy seven-syllable word I like very much. Can anyone guess what it might mean?"

Ashley, as usual, raised her hand fast and high.

"Yes, Miss Dean?"

"I think it means having big consequences. Like, when you do something, and the results are really important."

"Quite correct, Miss Dean," the doctor said. "Consequentiality. Important and significant results of an action. Now, Miss Brown is quite right. Thanks to Thomas's experiments, Flaxium presents us with a very tempting opportunity. By applying intense pressure, we could—if we wanted to—create an iceberg in the Atlantic Ocean right off the coast of Charleston. The water surface would cool, and because hurricanes are fueled by the heat energy of warm currents, an incoming hurricane might be chilled so much that it would be reduced to a harmless breeze. Hundreds of lives could potentially be saved. It sounds pretty good, right?"

Theresa nodded vigorously.

Dr. Flax clapped his hands lightly together in thought.

"But let us consider what else might occur."

Theresa felt her heart sink in her chest. She knew the answer, but she didn't dare raise her hand. She didn't want to answer or hear the answer. She knew where this train of thought ended. Her dream would end with it. Her father was looking at her sadly. He knew it, too.

He raised his hand.

"Yes, Mr. Brown?"

"Well, I'm only speculating," Theresa's father said, "but if an iceberg suddenly appeared off our coast, all the surrounding sea life would be shocked or even killed. Fish, shrimp, all the marine life of the low country would die. Our entire ecosystem would be disrupted and maybe even wiped out. Charleston, and many other towns along the coast, would be ruined."

Dr. Flax nodded sadly. "We scientists imagine the possibility of an invention. Can we create it? We measure its practicality. Who would benefit? But then—and this might be the hardest part of the inventor's job—we must consider consequentiality. We must be honest with ourselves about what our invention might do to the world—*even if we love it.*"

"B-but . . . ," Theresa stammered, "couldn't we . . . What if . . . Isn't there a way?"

"Not here," Dr. Flax said sadly. "Not in the Atlantic Ocean. Your father is correct. Creating an iceberg off the coast of Charleston might slow hurricanes, but the consequences to the surrounding marine life would be far too devastating."

Theresa desperately didn't want this to be true.

"You see, little girl? Your dreams, like my uncle's, will remain fantasy. Because my uncle is the world's most brilliant coward."

They all jumped with a start and turned around to see who had walked into the Big Zero behind them.

How could it be?

But it certainly appeared to be true.

Zachary Flax had copied himself a third time.

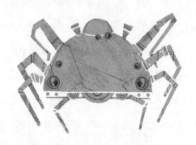

CHAPTER FORTY-TWO
THE ANSWER

G reetings, Zachary," Dr. Flax said with a sigh. "Thank you for coming, my boy. I owe you an apology. I didn't give you the programming you required, and I've never acknowledged you as my son, and for those two mistakes I am truly sorry."

The third Zachary's eyes glowed with golden rage as he stepped forward.

"I am not and never have been your boy," he said with icy cold menace.

George Brown moved between him and the children.

"Don't come a step closer," he said, and he meant it.

Zachary started laughing, even more wickedly than his first two brothers.

"Not to worry, Mr. Brown. I have no interest in you or the children. I'm not even interested in this laboratory. Unlike my two misguided older brothers, I seek something far more rewarding than replication or revolution. I seek *revenge*."

Dr. Flax reached out his arms as if he wanted to give Zachary a hug and tell him everything was going to be all right, but the third Zachary suddenly made a fist and punched a hole into the wall beside him. The water that had been flowing through the wall came flooding out. He ran across the room and punched a hole in the opposite wall, too. Even more water gushed forth, cracking more of the wall open as it came in torrents. Then he picked up one of the marbles of Flaxium from the table.

"Zachary, please" was all Dr. Flax could say before Zachary put his hand into one of the spouts of gushing water.

And squeezed.

The water turned to ice. Zachary, still staring at the doctor with absolute fury, was frozen solid. The Flaxium began its chemical chain reaction, freezing every molecule of water it touched.

The walls began to crack.

They all stepped out into the main hall of the laboratory and watched as springs of water burst violently from the walls and quickly turned into branches of ice. The laboratory began to crumble around them as trees of ice sprang in all directions, sprouting all the way to the grand fountain by the laboratory's entrance and then even farther.

The laboratory, once a lush subtropical garden, rapidly

froze, every petal of every flower covered in icy crystals. Theresa could only stare until her father grabbed her and held her to him to protect her and cover her from any ice shards that might fly in their direction. But in moments, the chain reaction was over, and the Paper Mill Mall that had become a laboratory of dreams had now become an enormous silent, frozen sculpture on a hot summer day.

Dr. Flax stepped up to the second-story guardrail and, without a scream or even a sigh, looked over it all.

"It's quite beautiful, isn't it?" the doctor said. He smiled and folded his hands behind his back. "If you ever need evidence that magic exists in this world, you need only look upon the wonder of ice."

Theresa's father was astounded by his calmness.

"But, Dr. Flax, your laboratory . . . *it's all destroyed* . . . This place was your dream!"

"Indeed, Mr. Brown. *Was* being the operative word in that sentence."

Dr. Flax stepped up to the frozen Zachary and knocked lightly on his forehead. Zachary's frosted and lightless eyes stared back at him, anger permanently etched onto his frozen plastic face.

"What an excellent demonstration to end today's discussion. As my dear Zachary has shown us, the consequences of releasing one's inventions into the world can be great. In the wrong hands, Flaxium has proven it is capable of destroying an entire laboratory—perhaps more. We must always be wary

that taking our creations out of our laboratories and into the public can have unexpected, if not devastating results. Oh, my dear Zachary, after I thaw you out and adjust your programming, we're going to have a long, long talk. I was so wrong to deny you the burden of being a son—you deserved a father to guide you, not abandon you and let you run completely wild."

"Aren't you sad, though?" Ashley asked. "Everything you've built is gone. You have to start all over!"

Dr. Flax shrugged.

"Repairs will be needed, yes, but Miss Dean, there is nothing more fun than starting over. But not today. You all need to go home and rest—that much is certain. I've missed several meals, so I must go in search of lunch. I don't believe Zachary will ever again grace me with one of his salads. Pity. He was a genius with roasted pecans."

"So that's it?" Jon asked incredulously. "No more labs? No more inventing? I won't be able to complete my masterpiece—my bubble organ!"

Dr. Flax started laughing.

"Listen to Mr. Cooper, everybody. His enthusiasm for bubbles has not been squelched in the least! Thank goodness, because your summer has only just begun."

"What?" Theresa asked.

"Inventors don't need such luxurious quarters as this. The size of one's laboratory does not matter. I happen to own a decommissioned yacht that I purchased from the US Navy. It has ample space for scientific experimentation."

Jon lit up. "Are you saying what I think you're saying?"

Dr. Flax smiled mischievously as they all began to catch on.

"Where would we go?" Theresa asked. "Away from Charleston?"

"The Florida Keys?" Ashley asked hopefully.

"The Amazon!" Jon said, jumping off his feet.

"I was thinking of heading north," Dr. Flax said, clapping his hands lightly together. "Icebergs may not belong in the Atlantic, but they certainly belong in the Arctic Sea. We could conduct our Flaxium experiments more safely up there. I also thought it might be interesting to try to bring cold water up from the bottom of the ocean to cool the surface with bubbles created from compressed air pushed through a long, submerged pipe. I imagine we'll require accompanying music."

"Hey, we could model it after my bubble organ!" Jon shouted.

"There's an idea!" Dr. Flax said, as if he hadn't already thought of it. "And if we are going to feed the barren regions of the world flavored algae, we should see how our crops fare under extreme conditions."

Ashley smiled and looked at her feet, not saying a word, but Theresa could tell she was happy to be back in the doctor's good graces.

"Do you think your bubble organ could play Disney songs?" Theresa asked.

"I don't know about that," Jon said, rolling his eyes.

"*Fantasia*," Ashley said quickly, lifting her head up.

Theresa smiled, and just like that, she knew she had her friend back.

Dr. Flax clapped his hands lightly together in thought.

"Of course, we'll need a form of transportation to get around when our little yacht can sail no farther north. There certainly won't be any roads to take us from glacier to glacier," Dr. Flax said. "What better way to get around than by mechanical spider? Especially if it is equipped with a set of skis compatible with water, snow, or ice."

Theresa grinned from ear to ear.

Dr. Flax clapped his hands once together loudly, startling them all.

"But first I must get my yacht in working order! Thomas, I'll need to program you with all the basics of marine engineering. Marie, you will be tasked with safety procedures and making sure we are all adequately prepared for emergency situations that may arise in the ice-cold waters of the North Atlantic and Arctic. And I will need swimming lessons, that much is certain. Yes, indeed. This should all take about a year if we don't dillydally."

Then he turned to Zachary and placed a hand on his frozen plastic cheek. Zachary's eyes had dimmed from angry gold to lifeless gray, but his vengeful scowl remained.

"My youngest son," Dr. Flax said. "I will program you to collaborate with others. You can achieve so much more with family and friends than on your own."

Then Dr. Flax let out a long sigh, full of regret but also

love. Yes, it was true, although Theresa could hardly believe it. Even though Zachary had tried to keep him locked up in a Pluff Mud Trunk, the doctor still loved him, as only a father could.

"Indeed, so much to do!" the doctor said, wiping a tear from his eye. "But first, lunch. An inventor must mind after one's own biological machinery. Thomas? Do you think you could improvise?"

"Um . . . I've never made lunch before, Father."

"No matter," the doctor said. "I think there is an extra loaf of pineapple bread in the kitchen and some freshly sliced pineapple in the LEATHER room. Pineapple sandwich, anyone?"

"Wait a minute," Jon said. "A year? What about my bubble organ?"

"And my algae experiments?" Ashley asked.

The doctor shrugged. "You continue your work until it is time to depart for the Arctic."

"Wait a minute—" Theresa's father began to protest.

"But I need my cool personal lab!" Jon said.

"And I have so many algae to take care of *here*," Ashley protested.

Dr. Flax chuckled softly.

"Do you know how many inventions I created in my parents' garage before I was even sixteen years old?"

Nobody answered, expecting this to be a rhetorical question.

"Forty-two!" he answered proudly. "I can assure you, a fancy laboratory is not necessary for the inventive mind."

"But my lab . . . ," Ashley said sadly.

"Yeah," Jon said. "I have nowhere to work at home. I don't even have my own *bedroom*."

But that was when Theresa felt the hole inside her fill with light and shrink to almost, practically nothing.

"I have the answer," she said quietly. "Our house."

Ashley and Jon looked at Theresa with hope, and Theresa looked up at her father.

"Can we, Dad? Can we divide the ground floor of the house into a three-room laboratory?"

Her father smiled. "I think that's a fine idea. It's certainly more agreeable than sending you off to the Arctic on a decommissioned Navy yacht."

"My house tomorrow, then," Theresa said proudly and with renewed excitement. "Nine to five. Wear something you're not afraid to get dirty. I'll provide a healthy and tasty lunch."

Dr. Flax smiled. "I knew the three of you would figure it out. Thomas? Marie? Let us leave these inventors to their own devices. Take what you like from the lab, colleagues. Even though it is frozen, I'm sure you can salvage quite a bit."

And then the doctor took Thomas's hand in his left hand and Marie's in his right, and the little family left to find something to eat.

"But we are going to the Arctic next summer . . . right?" Ashley whispered into Theresa's ear.

Theresa didn't say anything. Not yet. Not with her father

standing right there. She would need at least a year to convince him, but she knew she would eventually win him over. He would eventually see how important such an adventure would be. She was already envisioning the magnificent journey north. She could see herself riding Bonnie across fresh sheets of ice created from Flaxium. Yes, she would convince him. Her father would simply have to see that a trip to the Arctic in a floating laboratory was nothing short of an incredible, amazing, once-in-a-lifetime offer that she absolutely could not refuse.

ACKNOWLEDGMENTS

This is a story about a strong and creative girl who built a mechanical spider entirely on her own. But she finds she wants more. She wants to make her spider the best it can be, and she wants to take on bigger challenges, like combating climate change. To do so, she faces the difficult task of inviting others into her imagination. She must learn to collaborate.

Collaboration can be hard, but it's something I've embraced wholly so that my stories become the best they can be. I can only do so much on my own, I've learned. Luckily, I've been blessed with some strong and creative women to help me along the way. I'd like to acknowledge them here.

Sarah Davies, my literary agent who has recently retired from publishing to paint and sing, was instrumental in the early stages of this story when we weren't sure if it should take place in a hospital or a laboratory (I think we made the right choice).

Since 2019, three editors at Godwin Books have had a hand in the growth of this story—Julia Sooy, Rachel Murray, and Kortney Nash. Thank you to all three of you!

Most of all, I'd like to thank and acknowledge my wife, Rebecca. What a wonderful person to have in my corner when things feel out of my control (it turns out that, especially in publishing, things are often out of the writer's control). I'm so blessed to have her as a partner in this life. She encourages me to keep writing, to keep trying, and to not worry about the product and enjoy the process. Thank you, Rebecca.

I've dedicated this story to my three-year-old son, James, who loves robots. He likes to build things. He likes to dance, too. I hope he continues to build and dance. And I hope he is as fortunate as I have been to know so many strong and creative women. It's a very nice thing.